SPEAK of the DEVIL

MAYA DANIELS

VINCI
BOOKS

By Maya Daniels

The Broken Halos Series

Vinci Books

vinci-books.com

Published by Vinci Books Ltd in 2025

1

The publisher and the author have made every effort to obtain permissions for any third party material used in this book and to comply with copyright law. Any queries in this respect should be brought to the attention of the publisher and any omissions will be corrected in future editions.

A CIP catalogue record for this book is available from the British Library.

Paperback ISBN: 9781036706661

The EU GPSR authorised representative is Logos Europe, 9 rue Nicolas Poussion, 17000 La Rochelle, France contact@logoseurope.eu

Prologue

HELENA

Jolted out of a peaceful sleep is not a nice way to wake up. Neither is a consistent nudging in your ribcage by what feels like the hard edge of a shoe. Yet, this is the situation I find myself in. My ribs protesting, and my heart lodging in my throat, while memories assault my brain like a tsunami. The demon's sanctuary. Eric. Maddison. Us being surrounded by a sea of hunters, the fight, and finally me dropping unconscious while freaking out that Eric is the Prince of Hell. Like that was the most crucial thing in that entirely messed up situation.

"Good, you're awake." Michael's voice is enough to make me bolt upright.

"What the hell is the matter with you!" Snapping at him, I look around, trying to figure out if we are still at the demon's sanctuary.

I mean, of course, we aren't, but you can't blame me for hoping.

Michael is standing in front of me with his arms folded across his chest, scrutinizing me with disgust in his blue eyes.

At the moment, the feeling is mutual. We are standing in an empty room with just a chair in the middle of it, and brick walls surrounding us on all sides. No windows, one metal door, and a hanging lightbulb in the middle of the ceiling. The Archangel has some sociopathic tendencies it seems. That feeling that warns me of evil being near is going haywire in my stomach. Not seeing anyone else here, I ignore it the best I can. It's not helping me, and after the last day or so – depending on how long I've been out after Michael incapacitated me – I think that internal GPS is broken. It's just me and an Archangel here. Stupid intuition.

"I need your blood." The effortless way in which he says that makes me stiffen, and wariness creeps up my spine.

"How convenient for you." Darting further away from him, I try to see if there is a way out of here.

I see nothing.

Michael sighs, unfolding his arms so he can put his hands in the pockets of his pants. That's when I realize he has changed. By all intents and purposes, he looks ready to go to some fancy restaurant on a dinner date. I wonder if this is his way of trying to keep me off my game, keep me wondering.

"We can do this the easy way, or the hard way, Helena." He is walking around casually, and I move along with him, keeping the damn chair between us as if that will help somehow.

"We..." my words trail off, cutting that disaster before it happens, and I rethink what I'm about to say. "Where are we?" No need to mention Eric, or Maddison if I can help it.

"That's unimportant." Slicing the air with his hand, he keeps his focus intently on each move I make, mapping out every twitch of a muscle.

"I figured out your game, Holy one." Smirking at him, I

let him know precisely how Holy I think he is at the moment. He bristles, and I'm so proud of myself that the spreading smile hurts my cheeks. "You want to go to find Lucifer, so you decided to get your hands on the only ticket there, huh?"

"This is not a game, you insolent child!" Pressing his lips into a thin line and nostrils flaring, he glares. "I might've shown weakness by allowing Raphael to convince me to let you live, until now. But, I saw the inner workings of a Devine force finally." I almost sagged in relief at those words, but the glint in his gaze made shivers crawl up my body and numb my skull. "You lived so you can help me bring Lucifer down, finally. I've made allies, and his end is near at last. No more hell spawn crawling up into the human realm. No more power for the damned. It all ends with you."

"You are insane!" I'm freaking out inside, although no one can tell by the measured sound of my voice. My hands go to my thighs in a futile attempt to reach the guns that are not there.

"I am the only sane one in this situation. There is no other explanation why I let you live." A line forms between his eyebrows, and it pisses me off that it doesn't take away from his heavenly perfection." I need blood, and we are wasting time."

"I don't think so!" I dance away from him when he tries to grab hold of my arm. "If you think I'll let you do what you want willingly, you're nuts."

"As I already said, Helena, we can do this the easy way or the hard way."

Gravity does not affect the angels, or demons, the same way it does humans. One second, Michael is standing across from me with the stupid chair between us, the next he has me pinned to one of the walls staring me down. My body protests the force with which he slammed me against the wall, so I grind my teeth, stopping any sound from escaping, even while I'm screaming inside. Silver covers his irises, and his power pulses off him, making my skin feel like it's melting. Struggling for breath, I do the only thing that comes to mind. Lifting my knee, I hit him in the groin as hard as I can at the same time as my forehead connects to his jaw. I wish I were taller so I could've reached his nose, but seeing him drop on his knees and wrap both hands around his jewels makes me want to do a victory dance.

It's short-lived.

Bolting for the door, I grab hold of the handle and yank on it. It's locked. Michael's hand wraps around my hair, jerking my head back. After turning me around, he backhands me, the coppery taste of my blood filling my mouth. He uses his considerable size and strength against me, but nothing cripples me as much as the power that keeps rolling off him in waves. I try kneeing him again, but he proves that he learned that lesson by twisting his lower body away from me. A triumphant smile stretches his lips, and something in me snaps. He has a tight hold on my hair, but I don't care. Turning my back on him, my skull screaming in pain, I push my foot on the door, taking two steps up and flinging my body over his head. Curling my knees up, I force all my weight on his back and he slams his head on the door. The satisfying crunch of bone is music to my ears.

I know that I can't get out of here, for now at least. That doesn't mean I will give Michael what he wants easily. If he wants blood, he will have to earn it the hard way. Staring down at him, panting from the throbbing pain in my head where he ripped a handful of hair that is still tangled in his fingers, I spit in his face. The blood that filled my mouth sprays across his porcelain skin and mixes with his.

"There you go." Gasping for air, I bare my teeth at him. "That should be enough blood for what you need."

A furious roar shakes the walls around us. I should be afraid. I shouldn't taunt him like I'm doing. But all the should nots don't stop me as anger, confusion, and grief swirl inside me for the injustice of it all. And instead of trying to reason with him, or at least run away, I smile at the Archangel. He might hold me a prisoner and he might be stronger. But I will give him a run for his money. I have no doubt that I'm going to die soon. Might as well have some fun while getting there.

I don't know how many times we fought like that. In many of those fights, I would lose consciousness before I could stop him from taking more blood. Other times, Michael would make sure I was aware and helpless to stop him from doing it. Each and every time, he would get what he wanted, and then he would smile at me in a way that would kill me inside, little by little.

Hours turned into days, and the days turned into weeks. I floated between a world of pain and blessed darkness. Voices reached my ears. Some arguing, others purring, distinctly female, but I was beyond the point of trying to recognize them or understand what they were saying. Only one thought was now present in my mind.

'It wouldn't be long now. The Archangel would finally have enough and kill me. '

I started looking forward to that.

Chapter One

HELENA

Tightening up my arms and hugging my curled-up legs closer to my chest, I let my mind drift away from this place. My hair sways gently, tickling my forearms as I press my cheek to my knees. Eyes watering from the white around me, my thoughts race with everything that happened, and has been happening. After holding me in a dark brick room for what felt like an eternity, Michael locked me up in this one. The time is sluggishly moving, making me think it's been a lifetime that I've been here. My thoughts keep going back to Eric. I'm his mate. The only thing I know about mates is from the romance novels I've read in my downtime, and when Amanda used to daydream loudly about soulmates and everlasting love. It scares the shit out of me, and it makes my panic rise to dangerous levels, choking me. And he is the Prince of Hell. Time dragging slowly only amplifies my turbulent emotions. The only time I have a break from the anxiety and pain is when the Archangel comes.

Who knew a person can lose so much blood and still function?

At first, I fought him. I pushed with everything in me, like some wild animal that was cornered and fighting for its life. All my strength would desert me, and then Michael would manage to place one of his hands on my chest and send a current of electricity flowing through me. My muscles contracted to such a painful level that I'd pass out and wake up with poke wounds on my arms. It made me wonder how much blood he actually needed so he can enact his plans.

That's another thing. I thought; well we thought—Eric and I—that Michael wanted to go after Lucifer. Using my blood is his ticket to the depths of Hell so he can face the fallen angel. With each passing day, I'm starting to think that we must've missed something. Surely he had enough blood by now to keep that damn gate open for months, if not years. Yet, he keeps coming back for more, over and over again. A growl, okay more like a pathetic groan, passes my lips.

Closing my eyes to block out the white walls, ceiling, and the floor was not a smart idea. I feel like I've been locked in a mental institution while my mind is still sharp enough to scream for a way out. But every time my lids close, green eyes full of anguish and anger float in front of me. Unshed tears make my head pound with a horrible headache. Eric... Is it possible that someone can care that much about another person in just a few days? Better yet, is it possible for the Prince of Hell to care at all? Helena from not long ago would've said yes. This one that took residence inside me now doubts everything. I can't find it in me to blame myself. In just a week or so, my entire life has been turned upside down. Betrayed by those I called family and being hunted by my own people like some abomination will do that to a person. The sharp stabbing pain in my chest reminds me that I haven't gotten over it as I like to believe.

And, then there is Amanda.

My best friend's face with unseeing eyes is a nightmare I'll carry to my grave. Her beautiful face frozen in pain and terror, staring unblinkingly at the night sky. Her body twisted in unnatural angles at my feet.

All because of me.

The faint sound of footsteps coming my way alerts me of the company I'm about to have, and I blink slowly while I brace myself for what's to come. It's not like it'll be something unexpected. It's the same thing every damn day. At one point, I thought I must have died and this was me paying for whatever sins I have made in one of the circles of Hell. But then I remember Amanda, and I know at the bottom of my soul that I would've suffered more if that was the case. No. I'm still alive and wishing I was dead. How many more need to die because of me? Fucking angels, and fucking demons. All the fucking lives their war has cost us. That's a lot of fucks that I have no strength to give, yet they thump in my heart and mind insistently.

The soft click of the door announces my visitor.

I snort at my thought.

"Ah! I see you are awake, Helena." Michael saunters into my white cage, his cold blue gaze assessing me like a rat in a lab.

Not moving a muscle, I track his movement. There is no strength left in me to do anything but blink and breathe. I feel numb. Partly from the never-ending days, partly from my thoughts that torment me more than the Archangel will ever be able to.

A line forms between his perfectly shaped brows, confusion evident on his angelic face when I don't react to him.

My lips twitch, but I have no strength to smile. The white button-down shirt stretches over his broad shoulders, and it's tucked neatly into his black dress pants. The buckle of the belt on his narrow waist blinks at me, reflecting the blinding light above our heads. Silence surrounds us, and my breathing sounds too loud to my own ears. Michael looks at the tray of untouched food sitting just left of the door he used to enter.

"Not eating will only make you sick." Displeasure replaces his confusion. "Have you no respect for the life given to you?"

I blink lazily at him.

"Fighting me will not help." His face regains the emotionless mask. "Or do I need to resort to different means of motivation?"

My heart skips a beat at his words, and something lodges in my throat. I don't care what he does to me, but fear of what he might do to others makes my skull go numb. A shiver like icy fingers crawls up my spine. Uncurling from the small bed I'm sitting on, I lift my arm towards him. The bruises from so many needles being stuck there too many times to count look like some thermal heat signature map of a hidden treasure. Even with my fast healing, they seem like a permanent part of me now. The pants and tank top I'm wearing are also white, making the blue, purple, and green stand out more on my pale skin. *The guy is obsessed with white,* my mind supplies unhelpfully.

The door opens again, making me stiffen. Raphael walks in, and he takes a glance around the room, noting everything before his focus centers on me. His eyes narrow, and his lips press into a solid white line when he sees my outstretched arm.

"She hasn't eaten," Michael flings his hand toward the tray of food again.

"I wonder why, brother." Raphael replies dryly, walking further inside the room.

"Humans need food to survive," Michael says it pointedly, as if Raphael was not aware of that fact.

"They need other things, too." Raphael's face softens as he looks at me again. "Are you feeling well, Helena?" His mouth twists into a grimace. "Well, are you well enough, considering." His arm swipes around, encompassing the room.

I focus on him, Raphael moves closer and his fingers gently curl up around my still outstretched forearm. Warmth radiates from his large hand, and it feels like he is feeding me sunlight. It's the only word that comes to mind when the heat spreads through me, making my sluggish brain more alert. The dark thoughts disappear, and I find myself more aware than I have been in a long time.

"You waste your gift on that?" Michael spits the words angrily at Raphael. "She has no respect for life and should not even be alive. This is all your fault. Compassion has no room in some things."

"Are you certain it's the girl that has no respect for life, brother?" Squaring his shoulders, Raphael faces Michael. My skin prickles from the waves of power exuding from him.

Taking a step back, Michael gapes at Raphael. "You would stand against me for that?" An accusing finger is pointed in my direction.

"I do not stand against you, Michael." With a deep sigh, Raphael releases my forearm before walking towards the door, shaking his head.

"I didn't think so." Arrogance oozes from Michael while

he glares at me as if it's my fault whatever happened between the two of them happened.

Raphael opens the door, but stops before walking out. "Neither will I stand with you when you are wrong... brother."

His words make me look at Raphael. He's watching me intently, like he is trying to see my soul. Confusion clouds my mind, their cryptic conversation making my thoughts spin in hopes to figure out what just happened. And then, Raphael winks at me, one side of his lips lifting in a sheepish smile. My breath gets stuck in my throat and my eyes feel like they'll pop out of my head. Raphael walks out, closing the door behind him with a soft click. There is a feeling of finality in that sound that makes my blood rush like a flood gate is open through my body. The pounding of my heart is so loud in my ears that it makes me lightheaded. When I turn my gaze to Michael, he is watching me with suspicion on his handsome face. I don't know why, but I smile at him. Not a smirk, or arrogance. A genuine one that makes his eyes widen. And that's when all hell breaks loose.

An explosion shakes the place so hard I crumble in a heap on the ground. My head smacks the floor with a thud a second before everything goes black.

Chapter Two

ERIC

"Are you sure this is the right place?" Maddison scrunches up her nose like she's smelled something vile.

"It better be." My words are more a grunt than speech, but that's been my form of interaction ever since that bastard took Helena.

"Eric." She places her hand on my arm, and I jerk away from her, making her sigh. "I'm only trying to help. Letting you go crazy and causing more problems than we find answers hasn't proven very helpful in locating her. Who gave you this location?"

Okay, so I went a little feral and plowed through places and areas that I thought Michael might use to hide her from me. No matter what Maddison says, I can't find it in me to feel guilty. No one died, unfortunately, but it made the damn Archangel seem like he disappeared from the face of the earth. Fear that he took her to Heaven where I can't step foot dug a hole in my chest, making my logical brain take a hike. Few humans might now know about the existence of demons with certainty. Scrubbing my hand roughly over my

13

face, I push those thoughts away. I still can't find it in me to care.

"I don't know." Admitting that this just might be another of my fuckups doesn't sit well but it's better than doing nothing.

"What do you mean 'you don't know?'" The incredulity in her voice says it all. "I just summoned every person within range to come here, and you're saying this could be a bust?"

"Feel free to go home. Maddison!" Snarling, I whirl on her, forcing her to take a step back and eye me warily. "I don't give a fuck who it was. If there is a chance she is here, I'm going to take it!" Grabbing her arm, I shove her away, making her stumble back a few steps "Take your playthings and go home. I'll deal with this myself."

"You have lost your mind!" Clenching her fists at her sides, she glares at me, her eyes glowing brightly on her face. "I have let you be angry...hell, I'm angry for you! But don't you think for a moment I'm going to sit back and allow you to fuck up everything I've built because you don't use your fucking brain!"

"What would you have me do?" My roar shakes the ground where we are standing, but she doesn't even blink.

"Talk to me. That's all I'm asking." Collecting herself, Maddison walks up closer to me. "I'm not telling you to stop searching, or to ignore leads. All I'm saying is let's do this smart. Barging in fists flying has proven useless. I've let you do it for a couple of weeks, but it stops now."

I can feel my burning gaze on her, and anyone else would've been running for dear life by now. Not Maddison. She seems more enthusiastic with each word spoken, as if my rage doesn't faze her. Walking up even closer, she waves a manicured hand towards the building we are watching in the distance.

"Is this how you want her to see you when we find her?"

"That's a low blow, even for you." Turning away from her, I scan the area again.

"It's the truth and you know it. I don't know Helena that well, but I can't imagine her being all gooey when she finds out what you've done while looking for her. That girl cares more about others than herself. I thought you knew that."

"She is my mate." My fingers curl tightly, my claws digging holes into my palms. The warm blood trickling down my fingers soothes me slightly. Maddison's words are like a vise around my chest, making it difficult to draw in a breath. "He shouldn't have taken her from me. I warned him."

"No, he shouldn't have." Her softly spoken words make my body tremble. I want to believe it's from anger, but I know it's more than that. Fear claws under my skin because I'm terrified I'll be too late." "We will find her, Eric. I feel it in my bones that we are close."

My head swivels towards her. Maddison has many gifts, but when she feels a certainty for something, it should never be ignored. Searching her face, I find only truth. She really believes that we will get to my mate on time. Some unseen weight lifts from deep inside me, and the trembling of my body grows in strength. My legs can't support my weight any longer, and I drop on my knees, bowing my head.

"Oh, Eric." Maddison kneels beside me, wrapping me in her arms like when we were younglings and she would comfort me after one of my father's training sessions. "I know you're hurting, but we will find her. I promise."

"I cannot lose her, Maddison." Clutching her arms that

are wrapped around me, my words are rough and raw. "I will not live long if she is gone."

"I will not let that happen, cousin." The strength in her words feeds the sliver of hope she gave me a moment ago. "I may not know what it feels like to find a mate, but I will do anything not to see you suffer. If anyone has earned the right to torment you, it's me. I'm not letting that arrogant asshole steal my entertainment."

"Right." Her words bring me out of the misery I feel with a chuckle. She only hums, tightening her arms.

"So, what's the plan?" With one last squeeze, Maddison lifts herself up, reaching a hand out to help me to my feet. "We storm the place, or wait to see if anyone comes out first?"

"You're still sticking around for this one?" Glancing at her from the corner of my eye, I can't deny the hope her question is giving me.

"Walk away and what? Let you have all the fun?" Huffing, she moves and stands shoulder to shoulder with me, scanning the area. "Not a chance in hell." Snickering, she bumps my arm "Get it? Chance in hell." She giggles, but it sounds strained. I still appreciate it.

"I have lost my sense of humor." Snorting, I bump her shoulder with mine, "I was thinking of storming in there and grabbing her if that's where she is."

Maddison hums again, her head tilting left and right. "Michael went to great lengths to hide her whereabouts. I'm not sure we can just waltz in there if that is true. He will have security, and wards in place. If we get trapped in there, we're screwed."

"What is this place, anyway?"

The building looks deserted and old. The gray walls stretch wide on both sides of the metal double doors. No windows or other entrances are in sight, making me believe this is some sort of warehouse.

"My people tell me it's some sort of a research facility." Not taking her eyes away from it, she mumbles, "A laboratory, maybe?"

"He is hurting her." Growling, my teeth grind together at the thought. "I will rip his wings off his back, one by one and slowly, if one piece of hair is missing from her head."

"Look!" Maddison's urgent voice snaps me out of my murderous thoughts. "Is that him?"

"Yes, it is!" My feet are moving before I'm aware of it, but Maddison grabs my arm, stopping me.

"No! Wait!" Yanking me back, she tightens her grip when I try to make her let go. "We will follow him, and see where he is going. Don't ruin this now by acting rash. If she's not in this building, she might be where ever he is headed."

"Now you know why you're the brain of our operations." Pushing back the urge to go rip Michael's head off, I stop struggling out of Maddison's hold. "Just so we are clear, I have no intention of following him for days. If his next stop is not Helena, I'm coming back here and ripping this place apart."

"And I'll come to help you." She tells me distractedly and briskly moves towards our vehicle. Pulling her phone out, she presses a button. A second later, she speaks, "Don't lose him."

I follow behind her, jumping in her passenger seat. We don't talk while she maneuvers around back streets like she has been here a million times before tonight without having the headlights on. I learned not to question her about many things over the centuries. Anxiety makes my gut churn while my gaze sweeps around us, hoping to see the Archangel.

Occasionally, Maddison glances at her phone, but after we've been driving a while, my anger starts building.

"Don't tell me we lost him." Spitting the words angrily at her, I watch for any sign that she's hiding something.

"Oh, ye of little faith." Her words are mumbled as she takes a sharp turn, making me grab hold of the sidebar so I don't hit my head on the window. Slamming on the breaks, she slides between two cars, parking us on the side of the street.

My focus instantly zeros in on the Archangel a long way down the road, exiting his car. He straightens his shirt-sleeves, sweeping his gaze around him before walking up to a massive building on his left. The street seems deserted apart from occasional vehicles parked on both sides of the road. There are a couple of houses here and there, but none are close to the monstrosity that Michael entered. It almost looks like a hospital. I feel my eyebrows dipping low over my eyes.

"What is this place? A hospital?"

"A historical one is my guess. I don't think it's used anymore. Look." Pointing toward the doors with a finger, Maddison leans closer to the windshield. Thank the fates for our superior sight. "It has a plaque next to the door. It might be some museum or something."

"Well, let's go." Opening the door, I jump out, hearing her close the door on her side as well.

"Just one second," Maddison mumbles, her fingers typing on the phone with lightning speed.

"What are we waiting on?" Shuffling my feet with impatience, I study the building. "What the fuck is Michael doing in a museum? I think we should've stayed at the other place."

"We can go back there any time," Maddison says distractedly, not taking her eyes off her phone.

We wait here, my anger and impatience growing to a boiling point for over ten minutes. My fists keep clenching and unclenching at my sides. I had patience in spades until that she-devil walked into my life. She flipped everything head over ass with one look and a smile. Now, here I am, ready to self-combust at any moment while Maddison is playing solitaire on that fucking phone for all I know. Unable to sit still any longer, I take a step away from the car.

"I'm going in," I tell Maddison over my shoulder, sprinting towards the building. A blast of an explosion sends me flying back and drops me on my ass.

"And, let there be light!" Maddison sing-songs, clapping her hands in glee. I hear her footsteps before her face pops up above me. "You coming, or are you going to take a nap first?"

"Let's go!" Jumping up and shaking my head, I run. My boots make no sound on the pavement. Maddison follows a step behind, her laughter echoing around us. I might be in a rage because I'm desperate for my mate, but my cousin thrives on chaos. She is a mastermind of strategy, and more cunning than anyone I've ever known.

Chapter Three

HELENA

Someone is yelling.

I have no idea who it is, but my head is pounding like a church bell, and I feel nauseous. Gingerly sticking my fingers in my hair, I'm expecting to see them covered in blood when I squint at them, but they are clean. Pressing them just above my right ear again makes me wince in pain. A lump the size of a golf ball has formed there. No wonder I feel like my head is about to explode. *And who the hell is yelling?*

With a groan, I push myself off the floor, the white ceramic tiles cold under my palms. It was a bad idea to sit up because dizziness makes me sway, and turning my face to the side, I retch for long moments. Nothing comes out apart from saliva and acid from my empty stomach. Tears run down my face, making my vision blurrier than it already is. Sitting back, I blink fast to clear my sight, whipping my mouth with the back of my hand. *Where am I? And who the fuck is yelling?*

My hearing slowly gets better, the underwater sounds

that were muffled becoming clear at lightning speed. White walls and ceiling meet my perusal, bringing with it memories that flood my brain. Michael, drawing endless vials of blood, pain and despair overwhelming me, and the craziest of all, Raphael winking and smiling sheepishly at me. I finally lost my mind in this place.

"How dare you! You have lost your mind!" Michael's bellow coming from behind the closed door pulls me out of my thoughts.

"That is debatable." Raphael's voice is conversational, making me frown.

"This is what it comes to? You siding with demons?" A crash and a wave of power accompanies Michael's anger.

"I'm siding with no one." The door opens and Raphael sticks his head in, glancing around before spotting me on the ground. He nods once as if I've followed instructions and ducks right out. *What the fuck is going on here?*

"They will not have the girl!" Stronger waves of power make the air sear my lungs when I breathe.

"I think they will disagree, brother."

"Because of you!" Michael's voice sounds closer to the door now. "I will kill her if I have to, but she will not step foot outside that door."

"Then we have a problem, you and I." Confusion keeps me on my ass gaping at the closed door, while Raphael sounds like he is having a pleasant conversation.

"Get out of my way!" A sound like cracking thunder follows Michael's menacing words.

"Michael, stop! Don't you see what your actions are doing? The girl has done nothing wrong, to you or anyone else. What is your obsession with her?"

"She is not supposed to live! She should've died the moment we found her!"

"Yet, she still lives after you took her from her mate." Raphael sounds angry now too. "Why is that?"

"Get out of my way!" Michael spits angrily.

"Ah..." There is laughter now in Raphael's words, and I'm so confused that my head is spinning all over again. "I think you have company."

"Helena!" Eric's roar makes my heart skip a beat before it hammers erratically in my chest. "Michael! I'm going to rip you limb from limb, you piece of shit!"

My mind finally catches up with everything, and I scramble to my feet, slipping and almost toppling over in my haste to get up. Running towards the door, I slam my body on it with an oomph before fumbling with the handle. Yanking on it with all my strength, it doesn't move it an inch. Panic seizes my chest in an unforgiving grip.

"Eric!" Screaming his name, I pound my fists on the door like a crazy woman. The pain only feeds my frenetic need to get out of here. "Eric!!!"

"Helena!" Eric's voice sounds closer, and grunts follow it.

Flesh hitting flesh penetrates my panic, and I'm yanking the door with everything I've got. My entire body weight is not helping at all, until I hear a muffled grunt. Pressing my ear on the door and ignoring the numbing pain from the lump, I try to figure out what it was. Soft panting tells me there is someone else pressed against the door on the other side. Gasping for air, I will my brain to push aside the sound of fighting in the background so I can think. And then I remember.

"Raphael?" My voice sounds timid, and it pisses me off, but I can't do anything about it. "Raphael, please! Open the door...please!"

"Not yet, Helena. I will open it when it's safe." His

words are urgent, but fear makes me irrational. Eric is out there fighting alone for all I know.

"Please, Raphael!" Tears trickle down my cheeks. "If you let me go, no one has to get hurt." A voice that feels like part of my soul roars in pain, and I think something inside me dies. "Eric!" my fear-filled scream hurts my ears. "Open the door!" My throat feels raw, anguish fueling my need to be out there.

"Helena, stop!" Raphael grunts from the other side of the door. "If he sees you, he might get hurt." The words stop my yanking, and I stare at the door through the hair that's plastered on my face. "His focus is on Michael at the moment. If you walk out now, he will try to get to you instead of eliminating the threat first. Think!"

"Is he okay?" I want to slap myself for how stupid that question is, but I can't help it. "Is he hurt?"

"He will be fine." Amusement laces the words, and they don't sound strained now that I'm not trying to break out of here. "Your mate is strong, and he fights dirty." A chuckle follows that statement.

"I'm not sure who is the crazy one, you or Michael." Pressing my forehead to the door, I do my best to calm the jackhammering of my heart.

"After millennia"—he waits for the grunts, a crash and a bellow to stop before he continues like we are having a tea party— "sanity is a debatable thing."

"No kidding." Despite my fear, I chuckle, mumbling the words.

"No kidding at all." Raphael chuckles too, following it with a sigh. "I will need you to work with me here."

"What does that mean?" Suspicion crawls like spiders over my skin.

"I will get you out of here, but you must do as I say so

no one gets hurt." He waits a moment too long for my liking to continue. "Can I trust you?"

"You're willing to trust an abomination now?" My humorless laugh sounds bitter to my ears.

"I never thought you were an abomination, but I need your word, Helena." I can tell something has changed because he doesn't sound relaxed anymore.

"What's wrong?" Grabbing the handle again, I try to press it down. "What's happening?"

"If I don't get you out of here, they'll fight until one of them is dead. I guess I underestimated my brother's obsession with you."

"Let me out of here, Raphael! Now!" My palms, slick from the cold sweat coating them, slip away from the handle. The same one that also trickles down my spine.

"If I get you out of here, Eric will follow. They will both live." Raphael speaks urgently. "Your word, girl! You do what I say!"

Panic makes me hyperventilate, but I gather my wits about me. Hearing the calm and collected Raphael lose his cool does not sit well with me. "You have my word. Now, get me out of here!"

The door opens slowly, and through the crack, I see Raphael watching me intently, as if expecting me to grow another head. My heart feels like it'll break through my ribcage, thumping painfully fast. I can't remember how long I've been locked up in here, but I'm holding my breath at the idea that I will finally be free. One of my eyebrows lifts up when he doesn't open the door fully.

"When I open the door, I need you to stay behind me and walk towards the back of the hall. Am I clear?"

"Crystal." Clenching my fists, I let the pain from my nails digging into my skin stop me from running out.

"Remember your promise." His penetrating gaze narrows slightly before he starts pushing the door open.

I wait. My body coils up, ready to spring into action the moment I step foot out of here. Raphael blocks the doorway with his six-foot-five frame and broad shoulders. His focus is solely on me, and I know that if I twitch a muscle, he will slam the door in my face. Michael's power saturates the air rushing inside the room, causing my skin to burn like I'm slowly being fried. Shadows writhe behind Raphael like some scene from a horror movie. My nails dig deeper in my skin while I breathe through my nose in an attempt to stay as still as a statue. The sounds of fighting are too loud now that there is no door separating me from them. Nodding as if I've done the right thing, Raphael turns his back on me but doesn't move. Like a trained monkey, I walk up right behind him, wrapping my hand around the belt of his pants to let him know I'm planning to stay at his back.

Raphael faces the hall to our right, allowing me to slide behind him. He is too large for me to be able to see what is going on in front of us, but I follow his lead when he takes a step back. Shadows twist and turn around us like a living being. They cover most of the white walls and ceiling, making the hallway look like it's covered in fog. Slowly, trying to stay unnoticed, we inch down the hall. With a quick glance over my shoulder, I see the door at the end of the hallway getting closer with each step back I take. But then I hear Eric's pained roar, and I stick my head out to look around Raphael.

Michael has Eric pinned to the wall with a lightning bolt. The thick, crackling power is pushing deeper into his shoulder while his black t-shirt starts sticking to his body with the blood pouring out of it. The shock at seeing him so close, and him being in pain, cripples me. A pathetic whimper escapes my lips. But that's enough for Eric. His burning amber gaze locks on mine, and a shudder rakes through my body. This is not my Eric. He is, but he isn't. He looks primal and wild. A shiver, so strong that it makes my hands tremble, races up and down my spine.

"Helena."

My name sounds like a prayer on his lips before Raphael whirls around, snatching me in his arms and bolting out of the hall so fast that all I hear is Eric's enraged roar behind us.

Chapter Four

ERIC

She is alive.

I can finally admit to myself that until this very moment, I think I will never see her beautiful green eyes look at me. No matter how foolishly I convinced myself that I will get her back, somewhere deep in my core, I believed I'd be too late. I doubted, even after Maddison's words earlier gave me hope. Until that gaze locked on mine and the pressure that had been constricting my lungs from the moment she was taken from me lessened.

Helena is alive.

The bolt of electricity pinning me to the wall digs deeper into my shoulder. The pain of it searing my skin brings me back to the present, and the fucked-up situation I find myself in. Lifting my foot up, I kick Michael in the stomach, my boot crunching his ribs and bending him in half. My free arm swings, jutting my elbow up and hitting him on the underside of his jaw. His head jerks back sharply with an audible crack. With a roar, he stumbles back, and the bolt disappears. My shoulder is throbbing, blood pumping through the wound at steady bursts, but all I want to do right now is get to Helena. I was planning to kill Michael, the fucker deserved it, but I can do that the next time we cross paths. My mate is more important than my vengeance.

I call the shadows back to me, letting them sink back inside my body. The whiteness of the walls and floor blinds me for a second, but my feet are already moving. Michael is struggling to lift himself off the floor, flopping like a carp out of water. I might have broken more than a few of his bones, and bent one of his wings at an awkward angle. It'll take him enough time to stand up that I can reach the back door of the hallway. Raphael must have gone insane as well since he dared to touch her. I will break every single bone in his body, too, when I reach them.

"Come back and fight you, coward." Michael roars behind me, but I'm onto his pathetic excuse of getting me off track.

"Don't worry; I'll find you soon enough to finish what we started." Sprinting towards the door, I don't even turn to look at him. "You have my word."

My entire focus is that door. If I had the power to burn through it with my gaze, it would've been bursting in flames by now. My heart slows down, the rage turning into a cold and calculated calm. I am a perfect predator now. My breathing evens out, and all the sounds around me amplify. I can hear Michael's shallow breaths and the fast thumping of his heart. Every sound of pain he makes as the fabric shifts while he is trying to lift himself up. I hear heavy foot-steps thumping away behind that door. Much more substantial than just Raphael's body weight. He is still carrying my mate in his arms. I am going to break them slowly, I decide, as I strain my ears to hear what else is waiting on me behind that door.

"Raphael, go back. We must help him. Put me down, you asshole!"

Helena's husky words are like music to my ears, spurring me on. That she doubts my ability to get to her should hurt my pride, but hearing that stubborn tone in her voice gives me hope that my mate is not harmed to the point of no return. The door is almost at arm's reach when I hear Maddison's scream.

"Raphael, no!"

Everything around me slows down; it feels like I'm frozen in space and time. My outstretched hand is a hair's breath away from the doorknob, my fingers almost touching it. Madison's scream fades, and all the sound disappears a second before a blast hits the building in front of me. The walls cave in, the door bursting into pieces that fly past me, a few embedding themselves in my body. Flames like the pits of Hell have opened before me, swallowing me. I'm sent flying back until my back hits the solid wall that I was pinned to at the beginning of my chase after Raphael. My head cracks hard, and darkness covers everything.

Blinding pain makes my head throb, and muffled sounds float in and out of my ears. Distorted shadows swim in and out while I squint so hard my eyes must be slits. When I try to lift myself off the unforgiving ground, the pain in my limbs almost makes me roar with anger. *What the fuck is wrong with me, and where am I?*

"Eric!"

That voice will bring me back from the clutches of the abyss if I hear it. All the sound returns with a whoosh, and memories flood my mind, causing my head to spin. I forget all about pain and anger.

"Helena!" Jumping to my feet, something that seemed impossible only a moment ago, I look around for her.

When I don't see her immediately, panic squeezes my chest. Dust makes it impossible to see far, and flames crackle around me, they sound almost like they are chuckling menacingly at my anguish. There was pain in Helena's voice. *Is she hurt? How bad is it?* My mind goes crazy with the idea of her burning under broken pieces of the building. Running blindly through the collapsed walls and ceiling, jumping and tripping over bricks and plaster, I search for her, frantic with the need to hear her voice again.

"Helena!" My voice is so hoarse it scratches my throat and I almost cough out a lung. "Talk to me, cupcake!" *Please,* I scream in my head, but I don't dare to voice it. No need to frighten her.

"I can't even fucking die without you pissing me off." Her voice is weak and strained, but the relief I feel at her comment almost makes me drop on my knees and sob like a youngling.

"Keep talking." I have to clear my throat and swallow a couple of times to dislodge the lump. It's the dust that makes me feel like this. I will go to eternal sleep and still claim that to be the truth.

"I kind of don't feel like it at the moment." Helena coughs weakly. "Can you please hurry?"

Panic almost cripples me, but I stop to focus myself. Acting like a mad man will not help me find her faster. Closing my eyes and pushing my pain to the back of my mind, I slow down my racing heart. Wasting precious moments might cost me significantly, but I have no other choice. After an agonizingly long moment, I can hear her puffing short breaths not far to my left. With all my focus on her breathing, I open my eyes and scramble over everything in my path to get to her. My claws, fully extended, dig into bricks and tiles before finally reaching the spot where I can feel her. Surprisingly, this area is a clear circle, like a dome had been placed over it before the blast. No fires are raging, and no dust obscures my view. I need to blink a few times so my mind can catch up with what I'm seeing.

"Don't just stand there; I can't breathe." Helena wheezes, struggling to move her body.

In two strides, I'm at her side, and grabbing one shoulder, I fling Raphael's body off her. Helena gulps lungful's of air and struggles to lift herself up. Dropping on my knees next to her, I gather her in my arms and mold her body to mine. My shoulders curve in as if I can press her in so tight to me that we can become one being. Nuzzling my face in her hair, I inhale a lungful of her scent while my entire body trembles with the emotions raging inside me in a violent storm.

"Hey, monster boy." Her tiny hands clutch at me, telling me the feelings are mutual, no matter what her words say. "I'm kind of happy to see you."

I bark a surprised laugh, sounding more relieved than I want to show. "I'm kind of happy to see you too, Hel."

She laughs weakly as her hands slowly move over my arms, until they stop at something sticking out of my skin. Her sharp intake of breath presses her closer to me, making me squeeze her tighter in my embrace. Her pained groan at that almost makes me drop her on the ground.

"Oh my God; you are hurt."

"I'm fine; I promise. Just a few scratches and bumps, that's all." Now that she pulled away, I can't stop my gaze roaming over her face as if trying to memorize it all over again.

"You have pieces of wood sticking out of your arm and

leg, Eric." Her face is pale, and a vein throbs on her neck like a flutter of butterfly wings.

That's when I notice the changes in her. Her green eyes don't sparkle like they used to. There is a dullness in them that brings my rage too close to the surface. Dark circles under them make it more prominent. Her cheeks look hollowed out, and her skin doesn't glow like before she was taken from me. Not from the dust or the explosion. No, this is from the torment that she's been through. A feral growl sounds around us, making me crouch, ready to protect her, until I see her staring at me wide-eyed. The noise came from me, but I can't stop myself from doing it again. That's until my burning gaze settles on the Archangel's body not far from us.

"I'm going to rip him to pieces." My words are garbled, my tongue too thick in my mouth from anger.

"Eric, no!" Helena crawls faster than I thought her capable of, and on her knees blocks me from Raphael. Her hands are stretched in front of her, palms facing me as if that will stop me from killing the fucker.

"They hurt you!" I hiss at her, angry that she won't let me take my fury out on him.

"He saved my life, Eric." Searching my face, she must have seen my reluctance because she hurries to assure me. "Whatever happened that brought you here, I think it was his doing. He was getting me out and away from Michael when the bomb went off." Swallowing thickly, she looks over her shoulder at Raphael before her tearful gaze lands on me again. It pierces my heart. "He shielded me with his body from the explosion, Eric. I think he died to protect me." Her voice catches on her last words, and big tears slide down her cheeks.

Chapter Five

HELENA

I don't take my eyes away from Eric. He is crouched like a panther, ready to pounce. Tremors pass through his body. I know he is fighting with his control to calm the rage that's clearly written all over his face. If I saw him like he is at the moment a month ago, I would've either tried to kill him, or ran as fast as my legs would carry me. But things have changed. Lines were blurred between good and evil, and they had nothing in common with light and dark. Nothing in common with angels or demons. I don't know why it took me so long to understand this, and maybe Michael holding me in my white cage was a good thing in the long run. Because I finally know the truth deep down to my soul.

It has nothing to do with what you are. It has everything to do with who you are.

And the demon in front of me, his beautiful eyes turned into glowing ambers filled with rage at my pain is confirmation enough. As well as the body of the gentle Archangel that gave his life so that I could keep mine. A sharp pain stabs me in the center of my chest, making it difficult to breathe. He paid for the wrongdoings of his brother with his life.

"Please, Eric. Don't take your anger out on someone that doesn't deserve it. You said yourself that doing the right thing has nothing to do with what you were born to be." I try again to bring his attention to me. "Plus, we need to remove the wood from your arm and leg. You're losing too much blood at the moment."

After long moments staring so intently at me that I almost squirm on the spot, the green color bleeds through the amber glow. Finally, my Eric is looking at me with an unreadable expression on his face. My Eric. I have no idea when I decided on calling him mine, but butterflies fill my stomach at the thought. I almost smile at him, my lips freezing on my face when he sways, barely catching himself before he topples over. Panic gets me moving so fast I reach him just in time to catch him before he drops.

"I'm fine," he stubbornly says, but he doesn't move away from me.

"Yeah, I'm sure you are. Just like I'm fine." Waddling around him on my knees, I look at the sharp piece of wood that stabs through the front of his bicep, the sharp point sticking out from the back like some ancient spear. "I'm going to pull it out; just don't be a cry baby."

"That's what every guy loves to hear, Hel!" he tells me dryly, and I can't help but snicker at his serious face. "Just do it."

Eric doesn't take his focus off me. I can feel him burning a hole through the side of my face. I've shot the guy, twice! And he only grunted, pulling out the bullet with his bare hands. He heals almost instantly. The fact that he hasn't pulled the pieces of what looks like a door from his body makes fear crawl up my spine, and I can barely breathe. *Will I make it worse if I pull them out? Is that why he left them there?*

"Why haven't you done it by now? You could've healed already." Wrapping my fingers around the wood, I turn my head to look at him.

Eric's scrutinizing gaze travels from the top of my head to my toes tucked under my ass, and back up until it locks on mine. "You called my name."

He doesn't say it accusingly, or even angrily. It's a simple statement on his part. Me? I'm an emotional mess. My heart speeds up to a point I'm thinking I might end up having a heart attack. My entire body feels like it tingles, and a shiver makes me tremble. At this very moment, I know that no matter what happens, or where I am, if I call for him, he will always come. I have done nothing but bring trouble and distraction to him, yet he would do everything all over again without hesitation. *What have I done to deserve loyalty like that?* I haven't looked away from him yet so I nod, letting him know that I got the full meaning of his simple words. Without warning, I yank the wood out of his arm, almost falling on my back. He doesn't make a sound, but when I look back at him, there are lines etched on his handsome face, betraying his pain. I open my mouth to say I don't even know what, when a voice cuts me off.

"You are alive!" Maddison comes out of nowhere, stumbling in her haste to reach us. "Didn't you hear me screaming your names?" Not caring that Eric is bleeding all over the place, she bends down and punches his shoulder, glaring at him. "You cut down a few centuries of my life!"

Trying to hide the smile that is pushing my lips up, I bend over his leg, grabbing hold of the wider piece of wood. A dozen prayers float through my mind that he wasn't hurt worse. A small hand closes over mine, jerking back hard and pulling the embedded wood out of Eric's leg with a sucking sound that turns my stomach. Eric growls deep in his throat.

"That's for scaring the shit out of me," she tells him primly before she throws herself at me. "I'm so happy to see you're okay!"

"Thank you. I'm happy to see you didn't get hurt in the explosion, as well." Hugging her back, the words are choked out of me.

"We need to get out of here." Eric's voice stops the flood of tears that were threatening to come out. "I'm not sure why they haven't shown up yet, but the humans will be here any moment."

"It might have something to do with the bomb," Maddison says, plopping down on the ground next to me. Rubbing the back of her hand over her forehead, she smears dirt and ash on her porcelain skin.

"We will talk about the bomb and your carelessness when we get out of here." If looks could kill, Maddison would've been dead by the way Eric is glaring daggers at her. "You could've killed her!"

"Whoa there, cousin! That was not one of mine." Lifting both hands as if she's surrendering, Maddison shakes her head, her ponytail bouncing around her face in a cloud of red curls.

"What?" Eric and me both ask at the same time.

"That bomb," Maddison says every word slowly, as if we have brain damage, "was not one of mine."

"I'm fine, no need to check on me, or ask if I'm alive." A deep voice, calm and soothing, startles us all.

"Raphael!" My entire body sags when I see him peering at me with those cat eyes of his, checking me for injuries.

Crawling over to him, I grab hold of his hand, but he winces and I drop it. "I'm so happy you're alive."

"You might be the only one," Raphael mumbles, repeatedly glancing over my shoulder.

"Eric, stop it!" I don't need to turn around to know that Eric is either glaring or getting ready to pounce. "I told you what happened. Why would I lie to you?"

"Because your heart is soft and will protect even those who don't deserve it." His fingers curl around my shoulders, and he pulls me up, pressing my back to his chest.

"He saved me."

"That's the only reason his head is still attached to his body." Eric wraps me in his arms, but chills pass through me at his words. "Maddison, secure the Archangel. He and I need to have a chat after I take care of my mate." Raphael nods at Eric as if he understood some secret code that the rest of us mortals missed.

"Splendid!" Clapping her hands, Maddison jumps up. "Party at your house! I can't wait." Her enthusiasm makes Eric and I groan in unison.

Chapter Six

ERIC

After dumping Raphael in the back seat of Maddison's SUV, I fold my frame in the passenger seat with Hel in my arms. She doesn't protest, only curls up tighter onto my chest, and that scares the shit out of me. This woman is too softhearted for her own good, but she is a hellcat. To see her meek and looking lost makes me want to rage and destroy this entire fucking city with everyone in it. What have they done to her?

Tightening my arms around her, I bury my face in her hair. She smells of anesthetic and ash at the same time, but underneath all that is her sweet natural scent. It soothes some part deep in me that I wasn't aware existed. She sighs and pushes her face in the crook of my neck. I can feel her dry lips graze my skin when she speaks.

"Thank you." Her words are soft, barely above a whisper.

"For what?" Curling my hand on the back of her neck, I pull her back so I can look at her.

"For coming for me." Some feeling that I can't name

lurks in her gaze, making my gut tighten. "For searching for me…" she trails off.

"Don't ever doubt that, Hel." I make sure she sees my promise comes from the core of my being. "No matter what, I'll always come for you. But, let's not test that often, huh?" Trying to lighten the mood, I wink at her.

"Yeah, I have no intention of repeating it anytime soon." She giggles weakly.

"Rest now, I've got you." Pressing her face to my neck again, I thread my fingers through her hair. "You're safe. I'll wake you when we get home."

She mumbles something incomprehensible, but soon enough, her breathing evens out, and her body fully relaxes for the first time since I found her. Home. That's where I told her I'm taking her. The rest of the tension in my body calms with that thought. The rest of the drive passes in a blur of lights and sounds that I ignore. For the first time since she was taken from me, I feel tired as well. I haven't eaten, slept, or done anything else. Before I know it, Maddison parks in front of the glass double doors of the place I call home.

"Should I take Raphael with me, and let the two of you get some rest?" Maddison speaks softly, trying not to wake Helena. I want to say yes with everything in me, but uneasiness gnaws in my gut.

"We need to talk," the Archangel says from the back, my body tensing up at his words.

"You need to shut the fuck up." Growling through clenched teeth, I do my best to hold myself under control.

"Just because you have her here doesn't mean she's safe, Eric." With a heavy sigh and a painful groan, he sits up in the back seat. I regret that we didn't tie him up, but I didn't want to upset Helena.

"Let's hear what is going on." Helena shifts in my lap, and her voice is hoarse from sleep.

"You rest, Hel. I'll talk to him." I glare at the asshole for waking her up over my shoulder.

"It's not like I was running marathons, Eric. I'm fine. I could use some food, though, while we talk." As if to back her words up, her stomach rumbles and she presses a hand on it. "I could eat a horse."

"All of you go upstairs. I'll be back in a few," Maddison says, already buckling up in her seat. "Shoo, go! I'll bring food, but I'm not sure I can find a horse at this hour!" She snickers at her own joke.

I glare at her.

Rolling her eyes dramatically, she turns on the engine and looks at me pointedly. I'm in no mood to talk or deal with her antics, but I have a feeling I need to hear what Raphael has to say. Doing my best to not jostle Helena too much, I open the door and get out, kicking it closed with a loud thump. Raphael is next to me the next moment, but ignoring him, I stride towards the lobby. Helena doesn't ask me to put her down. I'm not sure I could, even if she did. It's as if holding onto her will somehow erase the last two weeks.

The elevator doors are open, thankfully, so we pile inside. Raphael presses the button for my penthouse, and I raise an eyebrow in question. He stares at the closed doors as we go up, ignoring me. I haven't interacted with Raphael much through the centuries. He is one of few that likes to stay away from the constant fights between our kinds. Which makes the question why he is here and willing to get his feathers dirty now more important.

Helena is quiet, although she's not sleeping. All three of us feel the tension building with each second that passes.

Whatever it is that Raphael wants to say can't be good. Not if he wants to tell it to me after he apparently went against Michael. The two of them are thick as thieves. What can possibly happen for one to turn on the other? And for a hybrid of all things. Maybe things are not as good as I always believed they are in Heaven. If I judge by Michael's actions, things might not be good at all.

The bell of the elevator reaching its destination breaks the silence and thankfully pulls me out of my thoughts. I'm impatient to get Helena inside past the wards protecting my place. Maybe then I'll be able to take a normal, full breath. The doors slide apart and just as I'm about to walk out, Raphael's hand clamps on my forearm, freezing me in place.

Dropping Helena on her feet, I push her behind me and my knees bend slightly by instinct. Raphael is still clutching my forearm, as if trying to stop me from moving. The door of my apartment sits somewhat ajar. Not enough to be noticeable, but sufficient for our enhanced sight to pick up. The air stirs around me, and Helena pops up next to Raphael pressing the "open door" button, stopping the elevator from closing. Lifting one eyebrow in challenge, she looks at me as if daring me to say something. I'm going to spank her for the attitude as soon as I have her safe.

Raphael takes my attention by tilting his chin towards the door, indicating he will be coming with me. I'm torn. I need Helena to be safe and stay back, but she has that stubborn look on her pretty face that tells me I'm shit out of luck. I'll just have to make sure she's behind me at all times so I can take the brunt of any attack that comes our way. I grab the Archangels hand, piercing his skin with my claw so his blood drips over the wards I have placed around my home. Doing the same to my hand, I watch them mix and feel the resounding shiver telling me he can enter. Nodding at Raphael, we both move towards the door on silent feet.

Helena steps softly, following me, and my heart fills up, bursting with pride when she comes behind me and her hand gently rests on my back. I strain to hear how many are in my apartment and where they are located, but I hear nothing. A frown pulls my forehead when we reach the door. A quick look at Raphael, I see the same confusion that I feel. Not a sound, a breath, or a heartbeat can be heard from inside the place. Apart from us three, there is no one else on the entire floor. Straightening up, I push the door open and stride inside.

No one is here.

I search the entire place within a minute, but it's empty. Is it possible I left it like that the last time I was here? I can't even remember when that was. I'm just walking out of my bedroom when I hear Helena's gasp. I've never moved that fast in my life, but I stop short when I get to the living room.

"Oh my God," she whispers, turning away from me, and I follow her gaze.

The color is drained from her already pale face, causing the dark circles under her eyes to be more noticeable. Her trembling hands are pressed to her lips, and her eyes are rounded in horror. She is staring at the hand left on the table holding a note between its fingers. Blood still drips from where the wrist has been separated from the arm. Moving one shaking hand, she reaches for it.

"Oh my God…" Repeating it, she points at the ring on one of the fingers. "Hector!"

Chapter Seven

HELENA

The horror of seeing my father's severed hand like some decorative piece on top of the coffee table breaks something fundamental inside me. No matter what Michael did to me, he never could've managed to damage me to this point. I feel my entire body shaking uncontrollably, and a bone-deep cold settles into my soul. Somewhere in the back of my mind, I'm aware that I'm in shock, but there is nothing I can do about it. I feel like a passenger in my own body.

I hear voices, Eric and Raphael talking in harsh tones, but everything is muffled as if my ears are full of cotton. Only the severe stuttering of my heart sounds too loud.

Thump! Thump-thump! Thump!

Long moments pass between each painful beat and numbness starts taking over. My teeth chatter, and the shaking of my body turns to an almost full-blown seizure. My knees give out from under me, and the room tilts sideways as my body goes down. The craziest thing ever is that there is only one thought in my head at the moment: *I'm going to hit my head on the table and it's going to hurt like a bitch.*

Strong arms wrap around me before I hit the floor, or the table as I feared. When I'm lifted in the air and pressed against a firm chest, I know it's Eric's. The warmth that radiates from him seeps through my cold flesh, and gradually, the sounds and feelings return with a whoosh.

"I'll bring water." Raphael's voice is laced with panic as he rushes towards the kitchen.

"Breathe, Hel," Eric murmurs in my ear, taking us to the sofa. "Just breathe. We will get to the bottom of this."

"He—" My voice cracks and no sound comes out.

"We don't know if it's his." The gruffness of Eric's voice brings back some of my sanity.

"The ring…" I tell him numbly.

"Could've been stolen and placed on anyone's hand." His fingers glide through my hair in a rhythmic motion, calming me more with each stroke of his hand. "Until we know for sure, I don't believe anything."

"I can go and check in the Sanctuary." Pressing a cold glass of water to my lips, Raphael perches on the table in front of us not far from the hand. "I'll look for Hector. Regardless if I find him or not, I'll be back before you know it."

The front door opens, and both men jump, Eric pushing me behind him and spilling water all over the place. The glass falling on the floor with a loud cling is followed by a thump of multiple bags.

"What on Earth…" Maddison's voice is high-pitched, making me wince.

"Close the door," Eric growls at her, turning back to me and pulling me into his arms.

"New problems." With a sigh, Raphael bends down and picks up the unbroken glass. "Someone left a gift." He points at the hand after he straightens up.

44

"Whose is it?" Picking up the bags of food that she dropped, Maddison strides towards the kitchen. "I'm guessing no one has an appetite right now."

"It's Hector's." I hear myself answer her, but I can barely recognize my voice.

Maddison's steps falter, but she regains her calm almost as fast as she lost it. After dropping the bags somewhere in the kitchen, she comes back and sits on the sofa across from us. She looks at the hand for long moments, her beautiful face not giving anything away. Then, those unnaturally blue eyes lift to mine. She looks at me for a long time, making me wonder what she is thinking. Whatever it is I'll never know, because her focus turns to Raphael.

"You said we need to talk. Let's hear it." Lacing her fingers over her bent knee, Maddison looks expectantly at the Archangel.

"I never thought it would get this far." Raphael looks defeated as his broad shoulders slump and he runs his hands through his hair, messing it up.

Eric growls something under his breath, but I elbow him to shut him up. I need to hear what the hell is going on before I can even try and deal with the fact that the hand still sitting in front of us is my father's. He tightens his arms around me and sniffs my hair in long deep inhales. For whatever reason, it calms him down, so I lean back into his chest.

"You both know," Raphael continues turning from Eric to Maddison, "that Michael has always been against the hybrids. I'm not even sure why he let me talk him out of killing Helena when we found her. But more than that, he has always been almost obsessed with luring Lucifer out of Hell so he can fight him."

"You mean kill him." I point out something that they all

skirt around. "I doubt he is looking for a friendly sparring match."

"Well." Raphael grimaces as if the words he is about to say pain him. "Who will be the victor in that fight is still up for debate. If they fight one on one."

"Okay, and he took me so he can open the gate. He should have enough blood by now to keep it open for years."

I should've kept my mouth shut. Maddison frowns, her eyes glowing brightly. Eric growls a deep, feral sound, and my entire body is covered in goosebumps from it. Even the hairs on the back of my neck stand straight.

"What else did he do?" The voice that comes from behind me is a thing of nightmares. It's almost as if Eric is speaking from deep in his chest, not his throat.

I shiver.

"That is why I made sure Eric had the coordinates for the laboratory." Raphael's words save me from replying.

"That was really you?" Eric's voice is still scary, but less nightmarish.

"Hmm, yes." Shifting uncomfortably, Raphael presses his thumb and forefinger on the bridge of his nose. "Things weren't supposed to go the way they did. You were supposed to destroy the laboratory while I took Helena away from Michael and brought her here. My planning went awry somewhere along the line."

"It would've been easier if you just told us that," Maddison says dryly. I can't help but agree.

"And you would've believed me?" the Archangel challenges back.

"We've always been at war, Raphael, but obviously you haven't yet learned that we are not stupid. If you came with an offer of bringing her back, why would we turn our back on it?" Maddison looks unblinkingly at him. "We might've thought it's a trap, but you know Eric. Traps are his favorite pastime. The way he was crazy with the need to find her, he would've taken you up on it even if he knew you were lying."

"What's done is done," I butt in because this is about to turn into a pissing contest. "What's in the laboratory?" An uncomfortable feeling swirls in my stomach as I wait for him to reply. I'm just grateful that Eric has been quiet and hasn't tried to go for the Archangel, yet.

"That's the problem." Raphael huffs, clenching his fists. "I don't know what's in it. Somehow Michael prevents me from entering it. I've searched for demonic wards that will prevent an angel from crossing, but I don't sense any."

"So, you figured sending Eric there was the best idea?" Anger overtakes my entire being at how nonchalantly they treat our lives, as if we are nothing. "Big fucking deal if a demon died, huh?"

"Why would I wish him dead?" Raphael looks at me with disapproval. "I just figured if we work together we both get what we want. I'll bring you to him, and he tells me what's in that cursed building."

"I find it hard to believe that you'd be willing to set me free just to satisfy your curiosity, Raphael. I might be young, but I'm not an idiot."

"There she is." Eric chuckles behind me, squeezing me tighter in his arms. "I missed that fire in you." Kissing the top of my head, I feel his breath stirring my hair. "She has an excellent point, Raphael. What gives?"

"You think he is commencing an army?" Maddison stiffens "You think we might have the start of a new great war?"

Raphael looks at each of us for long moments. His chest

rises and falls with even breaths. I can see the war he is fighting inside him in the storm brewing in those yellow cat eyes. Clenching and unclenching his fists, he finally comes to a decision. I don't even realize that I've been holding my breath until he exhales a long breath through his nose and drops the expressionless mask, showing us the fear that he feels.

"I think he is trying to kill Lucifer and tip the balance of all realms in the process." At his words, Eric goes still as a statue and Maddison gasps.

Me? I'm confused as fuck, and I still don't know if that really is Hector's hand sitting on the coffee table. Well, my confusion clears when Raphael speaks again.

"And I think he has demons helping him achieve his goals."

Chapter Eight

ERIC

"You are out of your mind!" The deceptive softness in my words is not lost on Helena. She shivers in my arms, and I tighten my hold on her.

"It actually makes sense," Maddison says while she looks lost in thought.

"You think that's how they found us when Michael took me?" Wrapping her cold fingers over my forearms, Helena is trying to calm me.

It's working. I haven't been able to stop touching Helena ever since I found her in that damn building. Just seeing her in front of me is not enough. My anger at feeling helpless when she was taken from me requires additional confirmation that she's really here. Her words finally penetrate my still enraged mind. I've been operating on it for so long now it seems I can't function without it.

"I cannot say for sure." Raphael lowers his eyes as if ashamed to admit he doesn't know everything. "It's from what I've overheard. Bits and pieces that I've put together.

49

When you usually sit on the sidelines and don't get involved much, everyone tends to forget you're there. It helps."

"What's in this for you?" Helena's question surprises even me. Raphael just looks at her wide-eyed. "If I've learned anything since my life went to shit, that's that no one does anything just because. There is always something there for them."

"I do not wish to see you harmed," Raphael says simply.

My possessiveness goes haywire. Helena only nods, accepting it at word value. I will need to have a long chat with the Archangel when she is not around. He can keep his angelic ass away from her. I've stayed quiet, mostly because I'm still barely holding myself under control. The urge to rip him to pieces courses through my veins with every beat of my heart for having his hands on her. The fact that he saved her does nothing to change my mind. She shouldn't have been there in the first place. The implications of the verbal bomb he just delivered feels like I've been sucker punched in the gut.

"This really complicates things." Maddison pulls me out of my thoughts. "It complicates them but makes perfect sense." Her intense gaze lands on me, and I feel its weight settle on my shoulders. *Don't say it,* I think to myself. "It was almost a perfect plan if he managed to keep Helena. Raphael messed up his plans big time."

"I don't understand shit, and since this is about me and my life, a little more info would be appreciated." Shrugging my arms off, Helena walks away from me, even when I don't want to release her. "Well? Someone better start explaining." Placing her hands on her hips, she looks at all of us expectantly.

"He needed your blood to keep the gate open. We thought he wanted to go after Lucifer in Hell, but obviously, we were mistaken. If he goes after him in Hell, fat chance that he will win that fight. Lucifer is at his strongest in his domain. Luring him here, however, weakens him and puts them on equal footing. From what Raphael is telling us, Michael is almost certain that he is going to win. Keeping you was his assurance to leave Hell in chaos. To tip the balance to that degree…he will destroy us all."

"I still don't understand. What do I have to do with it apart from keeping that gate open when I bleed." Helena looks adorable with the little frown on her face. I clench my hands, so I don't reach for her.

"You don't," I tell her, and that green gaze lends on me. "I do." Rubbing a hand over my face, I try to disperse the wariness that's starting to creep in slowly. "If Michael defeats Lucifer on Earth, someone must take his place in Hell. His heir." Understanding dawns and the color drains from her face, but I continue nonetheless. "And what better way to kill two birds with one stone, than to hold the heir's mate at your mercy."

"I'm not sure how far he is with his plans," Raphael murmurs, but I don't look away from Helena. "But we better do something to prevent it."

"This is never going to end, is it?" Helena's eyes flick to the hand on the table.

"We will make sure it does." Unable to stay away from her any longer, I walk up to her and pull her to my chest. "He might've caught me by surprise once, but I will not allow it to happen again. I will keep you safe, I promise. For both our sakes."

"Careful. I'll begin thinking you don't want to place your cute ass on a throne." She tries to lessen the gravity of the conversation, but her chuckle lacks humor.

"The reason I'm here should tell you I have no intention to go back there for anything, especially to sit on a throne."

"I wonder who placed the bomb." It takes me a moment to understand what Maddison is saying.

"You're sure it wasn't one of yours? It has happened before when your playthings don't know how to follow simple directions." All my focus is on Maddison, but I hear the crinkling of paper when Raphael picks up the note that we've all been ignoring.

"I'm sure," she drawls, pressing her lips in a thin line. "I only had two there with us, and they were both at the front of the building. I was coming through the back when I heard the distinctive ticking of the timer. It must've been there before we found the place and we somehow triggered it. We don't use timed bombs when we play it by ear. Mine were explosives. Just for a grand entrance, you know."

"Or there is another player moving pieces on the chess board." Raphael gets all our attention, and he lifts the note in two fingers. "Bring the girl or more body parts will follow."

"Okay, let's go." Helena is already moving, but I snatch her back.

"You are not going anywhere." Like fuck I will let her get in danger again. "We can figure out later who goes where. First, you need to eat and then rest. Tomorrow we can plan."

"Oh, like hell I'll let you lock me up here if Hector's life is in danger. You've lost your fucking mind if you think I'm just going to sit here while you play the hero." Spinning away from me, she turns to Maddison. "When are we leaving? I just need my guns."

With a groan, I plop back down on the sofa, tilting my

52

head back and flinging an arm over my face. "Life would've been too easy if you just did what I asked."

"First, you didn't ask, you ordered. Second, easy lives are boring and for humans. You are the Prince of Hell. You deserve someone to keep you in check." Helena's words make my lips twitch, fighting a smile. Maddison laughs at my expense as usual, and even Raphael chuckles. "So? When are we leaving?"

"You will be the death of me, cupcake." Her little growl makes my lips pull up in a full-on grin, but I keep my arm over my face. "First thing tomorrow morning we will make a plan. Then," peeking at her under my arm, I see the hunter in her shining through her eyes, "we hunt."

Chapter Nine

HELENA

I want to argue that we should leave now, and look for Hector. At the same time, I want to curl up in a ball in the closet and pretend none of this happened. A sense of déjà vu makes me hesitate before arguing my point. This is the exact same feeling I had before Michael took me. I spent a long time wishing things would go away or wanting to pretend that they didn't happen.

These people, or Archangels as the case may be, know me too well. They molded me into the person I am today, regardless if they like it or not. I wonder if everything is done on purpose to keep me confused, running in circles like a dog chasing its own tail. If that truly is the case, I don't blame them. They played me for a fool. I have no doubt that I've reacted just as they expected me to. So how about we change the game?

I am a hunter. It makes no difference what I'm hunting, and I need to keep that in mind. When it is just me and my life in question, I do have a problem turning on an Archangel. But, Michael changed the rules. He went after those I love, and that changes everything. Maybe it's time he meets the hybrid he hates so much. Not Helena the hunter.

"Okay," I tell Eric, unable to look away from him.

His long legs are stretched out in front of him, the muscled thighs testing the elasticity of his leather pants. One of his forearms is flung over his face. The t-shirt he is wearing has lifted up, exposing part of his defined abs, just enough to give me a glimpse to tease me. My hormones are messing with my head at the sight of him like that.

"Did you say okay?" He lifts his head up to look at me properly, and the shocked look on his face is comical.

"I'm all for hunting. If I need to wait until tomorrow, that's fine. It's not like we can change anything if that really is Hector's." Pointing in the direction of the table, I do my best not to look that way. "And I really am hungry. Now that the initial shock has worn off, I need food and a shower. In that order."

Raphael jumps up, walking briskly towards the kitchen and starts rummaging through the bags of food. Maddison moves after him after picking up the hand and taking it somewhere in the apartment. After facing each other for a while longer, Eric stands up and, tucking me under his arm, leads me there too. We spread the plastic containers on the long dining table, and without a word we attack the food like a pack of starving wolves. It's a companionable silence, and judging by the relaxed shoulders and missing frowns around the table, nobody feels awkward because of it.

I can't stop the soft moan when I bite into the cheese and herb breadstick. If I told Maddison what I crave, I couldn't have picked better. Noticing Eric's penetrating gaze, I do my best not to look at him. Dipping the breadstick in the warm marinara sauce, I bite off a large chunk again. It might not look very pretty, but after that first bite, I feel like a hole has been opened in my stomach. I wasn't aware of how hungry I was until that moment. The aroma spiraling up from the pasta dishes, especially the lasagna, only makes my mouth water more. Inhaling as much food as I can possibly fit inside me, I feel my head dropping. After the second time, I jerk back to stop from face planting into the table, Eric pulls my arm and drags me to the bedroom.

I follow at his heels without argument, the soft conversation between Maddison and Raphael fading behind me. He leads me through the bedroom towards the open door of the bathroom, but I pull on his hand to stop him when we pass the tallboy. Reaching my hand out, I glide my fingers over the metal of my guns. They are neatly placed on top of it just like the last time I saw them.

"Come." Eric tugs on my hand gently. "You need a shower before you fall asleep. You can play with your guns tomorrow."

I follow him without a word. He is right; I just don't want to tell him that. Otherwise, he will get more arrogant than he already is. From the moment he figured out I'm his mate, his protective side became overbearing. I'm not used to people fussing over me the way he does. Hector was protective, yes, but he would send me out in the middle of a horde of demons without blinking an eye. Did he have more faith in me, or did he hope I'd eventually end up dead?

All my thoughts of Hector and my ability as a hunter disappear when we enter Eric's bathroom. The sight of it relaxes me to the point that my legs feel too heavy to move. Standing still, I watch Eric as he turns around and studies me for a moment before his fingers wrap around my shoulders. He glides his hands over my arms gently, the rasp of his calloused fingers bringing a familiar fluttering inside my lower belly. The intent focus he has on me tells me that he is waiting for a sign. It eludes me what he is expecting to see, but I stand there and allow the perusal.

Without a word, he pushes his fingers under the tank top I'm wearing and slowly pushes it up my torso. Everywhere his skin touches mine creates little pebbles, electricity streaming through me and spreading warmth inside me that was missing. Lifting my hands up and helping him pull it over my head makes my hair fly around my face, covering my view of him. His hands push it back after he drops the tank top at our feet. I have no bra—the Archangel was not very concerned with trivial things like that—and my nipples turn to stiff points. Eric's gaze travels from my face to my breasts for a fleeting moment but comes back up too fast for my liking.

I have missed him. Actually, that's an understatement now that I'm out of that damn place and away from the asshole Archangel. I more than missed him. The feeling spreading through my entire being at having him so close takes my breath away. But he does nothing else. He continues to undress me, pulling my white cotton pants over my hips. With one hand on his shoulder to keep my balance, I lift one leg up, then the other, while Eric kneels in front of me. There is unmistakable hunger on his handsome face as his hands glide up my legs and take hold of the white underwear that is left. He pulls that down too, his eyes flashing amber for a second before he stands up again.

We don't talk. I expect lectures or him trying to convince me to stay behind, but none of that happens. Eric takes my hand and guides me to the shower. I appreciate his presence and the time he is giving me to just be. Although, I'm a little surprised that he didn't undress while I'm standing in front of him in my birthday suit. Still, I track every movement he makes. The shower turns on and warm water slices through my body, making me sigh in content and close my eyes. Eric tilts my head back, standing under the spray of water fully dressed and starts washing my hair. With gentle and caring movements, he cleans every inch of me, his hands caressing me as if I'm made of glass and will shatter at any moment. Unshed tears burn my eyes, and I'm grateful for the water droplets that hide them when they spill over.

When he is done, he wraps me in a thick towel and dries my hair with another. The anticipation of his touch, of him being inside me, keeps me on edge. He guides me back to the bedroom, pushing me gently on the bed and pulling the sheet over me. Disappearing again in the bathroom, he comes back out after a moment wearing only black boxer briefs and slides under the sheet, wrapping his strong arms around me and pulling me over his chest.

"Sleep now, Hel. I got you," he murmurs in my hair and sighs as if the weight of the world is on his shoulders. Maybe it is.

He moves his hand up and down my back in soothing motions, and without any other words spoken, I drift off to sleep. I have never felt safer or more cared for than at that moment.

Chapter Ten

ERIC

The gliding of a soft hand over my chest pulls me out of sleep. Without opening my eyes, I tighten my arms, taking a deep breath and inhaling the scent of Helena. The hand on my chest stops moving, and I can feel her heartbeat quicken.

"I didn't mean to wake you up." Her apology is softly spoken, her breath tickling my skin.

"I shouldn't have been asleep. Having you back made the lack of sleeping finally catch up with me." Kissing the top of her head, I do my best not to roll on top of her and bury myself inside her.

"Everyone needs sleep, Eric. Even you." Poking me with a finger, she lifts herself up and looks down at me. "Even the Prince of Hell."

I keep my eyes closed, my gut tightening at her comment. I've been dreading this conversation. Helena was raised to hate demons, her only goal since she can remember was to eliminate me and my kind from the face of the Earth. And here I am. Her mate. The demon of all

59

demons—after my father, of course. Does she hate me for it? Will she resist the bond we have because of who I am? I have been reckless and wild, taunting the fates with each breath I take, but I find myself a coward in front of this woman. I'm not even sure that I'm breathing after her comment.

"So…" Taking a deep breath, Helena releases it slowly. "Prince of Hell, huh?" She chuckles weakly. When I don't say anything, she thumps a fist to my chest. "Eric, stop playing dead. It's annoying." Huffing a breath, she flings herself away from me, and the coward that I am, I let her.

"I don't know what to say to that, Hel." Still keeping my eyes closed, I press on them with my thumb and forefinger to elevate the headache that is building there already. "If I could change who I am for you, I would do it in a heartbeat. Alas, I can't." Gathering as much courage as I can, I finally look at her. "I am what I am."

She is standing naked next to the bed, intently watching me with that penetrating green gaze. She's searching my eyes as if she's trying to find all the answers there. Or maybe trying to find something that she feels I'm hiding. I have no clue what it is, but I let her see me. Allowing all the masks and walls that I've built around me to fall down so she can see her mate for what he is. A scared coward.

"The crazy thing is, I actually believe that you would change it if you could." Her breathing speeds up.

"I would."

Reaching a hand towards my face, she glides her fingers over my skin, tracing it. We stay locked in a staring match, and I can't help but feel pride in her. She has come a long way from the confused girl I met not long ago. That girl is long gone. The woman standing in front of me does not let me shy away from what she demands to know. I hate every-

60

thing that happened to her that made her into who she is this very moment, but I can't help loving her more for it. She must've seen something in my eyes because she snatches her hand away from me like I've burnt her.

"You don't like what you are." It's a statement, not a question.

"I don't like what's expected of me because of what I am." Lifting myself off the bed, I stand in front of her. "There is a difference."

"What does that mean, Eric?" She walks into my closet, coming out of it pulling one of my shirts over her head. "All of you are talking to me like I'm some sort of know-it-all, and your words are supposed to make sense." She jumps on the bed curling her legs under her, totally unaware how seeing her in my clothing affects me. I'm barely keeping myself from pouncing on her, but she keeps talking. "I'm the pink elephant in the room, the abomination, yet all of you sound like you're talking gibberish. The Order does that shit, you know. They give half-truths and incomplete information. Just enough to keep you on a short leash. It's starting to piss me off."

"My father has been honing my skills, and training me to stand beside him when I come fully into my powers from the moment I could walk. He thought just because I am his son, I would follow blindly and do everything he says. He got his rude awakening when I was finally able to leave his realm. I followed Maddison here, and I've never looked back. That was centuries ago."

"He wanted you to stand beside him, and do what exactly? Kill humans? Angels? Think of me as naïve, but I don't really understand." Helena's words are soft, and I'm breathing easier because she's not screaming at me and running away. Yet. She's not doing that, yet.

"He fell from grace because he thought everyone should have free will. Let's just say that his wishes bit him in the ass. The seven sins are not a made-up tale to control the masses. They are part of human nature. Free will to make their own choices can be a blessing on those with a kind and compassionate heart. It is a curse when it is a twisted mind or heart. Everyone that is not pure enough to ascend to Heaven is sent down to Hell. They don't change simply because they exchanged one realm for the other. Skirmishes, takeovers, fights, and wars are almost an everyday occurrence. My father was strong enough to control them all, but with time, the numbers were increasing. Modern times lead more and more to temptation, and they kept filling his realm. They still are." Sitting next to her, I take her hand in mine, lacing our fingers together, and warmth spreads through me when she doesn't pull away. "So, I left, and he is dealing with it on his own. He has his underlings to help him out, but they are not powerful enough to keep a large number of demons under control. That's why we are dealing with so many rogues lately. I refuse to stay in Hell, but I'm helping in my own way from here. It's not enough for him, but he has to deal with it. Fortunately, he hasn't tried to force my hand and push me to go back. I'm not sure he wants to start a war with his own son. It's also a pride thing. If he can't control his son, how can he control the realm? So, he plays along with me turning my back on everything. If he finds out about you, however, I'm not sure a war can be prevented. The angels are not helping either with their consistent poking at him. Especially with what Michael is trying to do now."

"I know I said it jokingly yesterday, but I'll ask again." Helena tilts her head, making her hair spill over her shoulder "Anyone in your shoes would grab the chance to sit in a place of power. And here you are, running away from it. You're telling me he needs you to control Hell, and you refuse only to stay here on Earth and fight the rogues that wouldn't have been here in the first place if you stayed where you belong." Tightening her hand in mine, she tugs on it gently. "I'm not accusing you of anything, Eric. I'm trying to understand."

"I can't stay there, Hel. He is not some kind and understanding person. I don't blame him for what he has become because dealing with all that since the beginning of time would turn anyone insane. He is cruel and merciless because that's what he needed to be. I'm not sure he knows how to be anything else after so long. Now, with everything that happened with the Archangels, I can't help but wonder if it's the years making all of them lose it. Earth has always been their playground. Humans, as fragile as they are, are what's holding everything together. Heaven feeds off of their prayers and worship, and Hell feeds off of their fears and sins. I'm more useful here than I am sitting there to soothe my father's pride."

"And what happens if Michael succeeds in killing your father?"

"I will have no other choice but to take his place." Not taking my eyes away from her, I hold my breath to see if she understands what I'm implying.

"If you don't?"

"The gate will disappear, causing Hell and Earth to merge into one."

Chapter Eleven

HELENA

I watch Eric, and my heart is breaking at the uncertainty I see in him. This strong man that will stop at nothing to protect me, even from myself, is looking at me at this moment like I'm his executioner or his savior. That doesn't sit well with me. But neither does the fact that his words give me a pause. It's not so much about what he is saying, it's about everything between those lines.

If Michael succeeds in luring Lucifer to Earth, and killing him, we are screwed. That means Eric will be going to Hell, if we don't want a clusterfuck of epic proportions to hit the human realm. If he has to do that, I have no doubt he will want me to go with him. Even now, I feel our connection pulsing in the center of my chest, tying me to him irrevocably. That part of me that is a demon almost purrs at the idea. A messed-up sense of belonging rears its ugly head inside, freaking the hell out of me—pun intended. The half angel part rebels at even considering such a blasphemous thought. To say that I'm conflicted is the understatement of the century.

"You are not running away," Eric says quietly, his thumb rubbing slow circles on the back of my hand.

Snorting ungracefully, I shake my head. "I'm way past the running part, monster boy. I'm just lost for words and don't know what to say, or think for that matter."

"Then say nothing, Hel." Cupping my face in his warm palm, he searches my eyes. "Let's take it one day at a time. I will not let my father, or any angel, stand in my way of having you. If Michael thought my father was his biggest problem, he doesn't know what he got himself into. I will bring Heaven and Hell down before I let them take you away from me, or I'll die trying. You need to know that without any doubt."

I feel the slight tremors in his hand, although he is trying very hard not to show how much this conversation is affecting him. Or maybe it's the uncertainty of what my reaction will be that's making him seem almost human at this very moment. All that flies out the window when he lets me see the vulnerability in his eyes. It rips me apart, and my vision gets blurry from unshed tears.

"Oh, Eric…" Grabbing his face in both my hands, I kiss him like a woman dying of thirst.

It's as if he lost the control he has been holding onto at that. His arms wrap around me, crushing me to his lap, while he devours my mouth. A desperate sound rumbles from his chest, spurring me on. The feel of him, the taste of his kisses, slam into me like a Mack truck, and I lose myself in everything that is Eric. His hands roam my back, squeezing me tighter to him. Wrapping my fingers in his hair, I cling to him like my life depends on this, on having him as close as possible.

Eric pulls away too soon for my liking, making me whimper at the loss of his lips on mine. He starts kissing a hurried trail down my neck, erasing the stinging from his bites with his tongue. He pushes his shirt that I'm wearing over my head and flings it away, latching onto my nipple. The moans and panting coming from both of us make my entire body tremble in his arms. I can feel his muscles twitching under my fingers, like he is trying to slow down. I'm having none of that. I'm too desperate for him at the moment to allow him to take his time. Not giving him a chance to realize my intentions, I shove my hand down the boxer shorts he is still wearing, pulling his hardness out and impaling myself to the hilt in one jerk of my hips. Hissing, Eric grabs my hips in a bruising hold and his amber gaze locks on mine.

"I will hurt you." Growling through clenched teeth, he fails to stop himself from grinding between my legs.

"I don't care, Eric. I need you." My words are more a moan than a demand, but the look on his face gives me shivers. Pure, undiluted hunger.

He lifts up and slides both his hands under my ass, and when he grabs it firmly, I wrap my legs around his narrow waist. Placing one knee on the bed, Eric positions his hands to hold me half suspended in the air, my head thrown back, my nails digging into the skin of his arms. I'm so wet at the moment I can feel his groin and thighs sleek with my juices. And then, he pumps his hips in a punishing tempo. I can't do anything else other than hold on to him for dear life and moan at the pleasure shooting through every part of my body.

The sound of skin slapping on skin mixes with my desperate moans. Eric is producing sounds deep in his chest that would sound terrifying if I wasn't so lost in the feel of his hardness stretching me and filling me up so completely that I can't even remember my own name. All I know is him. All I can feel is how he takes control of my body. And I never want this to end. At this very moment, if he asks me to go to Hell, I would say yes a million times. But that's not Eric. He doesn't take advantage of my delirious need of him, of feeling alive. He just gives me what I need, what we both need.

The tightness in my lower belly stretches, and I can feel the early spasms starting in my channel. I'm so close to climaxing, intangible words spill from my lips. Eric speeds up, pumping his hips even faster than before.

"Kiss me." His deep voice reaches my ears, his growled words making goosebumps cover my entire body.

Lifting my head up with a lot of effort, I kiss him.

When my tongue tangles with his, a feral sound comes from him, driving me insane. Twisting around, he pushes me on the bed and presses his weight on me. The fast pumping of his hips doesn't falter. I can feel his sack slapping my ass and it just adds to the insanity as I desperately chase the bliss. Sweat makes our skin stick to each other's, and the scent of sex fills my lungs. The rubber band that has been stretching inside me finally breaks. The scream that is ripped from me is quickly followed by a roar that shakes the windows. The entire building will know what we are doing, but I can't find it in me to care. I feel the warmth bathe my insides with each pump of Eric's hips as his cum fills me to the brim. The liquid pours out of me, coating my thighs and the bed underneath me, yet he doesn't stop. Another orgasm hits me, and my raw throat can't produce a sound. With my mouth open in a silent scream, I cling to him until finally we both relax and slump on the bed.

"I missed you," Eric rasps, kissing my neck.

I make a sound—something between a huff and a laugh—at his words. "I wouldn't have guessed, monster boy." His chuckle brings a stupid smile to my face.

Chapter Twelve

ERIC

Everything in me balks at the idea of letting Helena out of this room. Having her underneath me, her breath tickling the skin of my shoulder, makes me want to jump and ravish her all over again while I hide her from the world. I know we have to move, so although I'm still hard as a rock and inside her, I lift myself up on my forearms to look down at her.

"Eric…" The look she gives me tightens my gut, and I kiss her to stop whatever words are about to come out.

Reluctantly releasing her mouth and giving her a gentle press of lips, I sigh. "One day at a time, Hel. That's all I'm asking."

"They're not joking when they say the devil comes after everything you've ever wanted, huh?" She smiles sheepishly at me.

A burst of surprised laughter is ripped from me, and the shaking of my body makes her moan, her channel spasming around my cock. I give her a warning growl, but she shrugs unapologetically.

"I've missed you, too, it seems." Her hands glide over my shoulders and down my arms, making every muscle she comes in contact with twitch in anticipation. "But we need to start planning. Actually…" a devilish smile brightens her face, "first, we need to go see if the Archangel had a conniption after our performance."

Pressing her hands on my chest, she gives me a push, and I roll off her. I'm momentarily startled at the strength she displays, but I keep my mouth shut because she doesn't look like she did it on purpose. Oblivious to my stunned face, Helena lifts herself up and disappears in the bathroom, her naked body distracting me from the shock. After a moment, I hear the shower turn on, but can't get myself to move. She was so tired last night, and maybe that's why she looked almost broken. As much as I dread hearing what she's been through, I need to know every detail. She was strong before, but something has changed in the time she was gone. She flipped me off her as if I was a blanket, not two hundred and eighty pounds of muscle on top of her. All that without a clue of what she's done.

I think back to the night before. Raphael's unconscious body was on top of her when that damn bomb went off. She could barely breathe and was asking for help, which was very unlike her. Was it because she was stunned from the blast, or because of exertion? If she is aware of the changes in her, she sure didn't mention it. I decide to let it play out as it will. I'm going to keep an eye on other changes, if she shows any. I clench my teeth, trying hard not to bite the inside of my mouth. If that fucker has done something to her to cause this, our fight is far from over. I won't stop until he is dead.

The water cuts off. When the sound of a blow dryer dies down, I jump off the bed. I don't want her to notice my turmoil. There are more pressing matters to deal with. At the end of the day, we will deal with whatever it is that caused this change together. It might not be a bad thing with everything that's waiting for us. I told her one day at a time, but like fuck I'm going to let her get away from me. She is mine, and with time she will know that for a fact. I just need to tread lightly, or she will fight me every step of the way.

I take my own shower, but not before pulling her to me and kissing her senseless when we pass each other. When we are both dressed, I'm rethinking my willingness to let her out of the room, but she gives me a stern look while holstering her guns. That makes me clamp my mouth shut, begrudgingly following her to the living room. The sway of her hips as she walks in front of me make my pants feel tight. I don't think I'll ever get enough of this woman, even if I keep her locked in my bedroom for a few centuries.

"Oh, good! You are awake," Maddison drawls, mischief dancing in her gaze.

"Yup!" Helena answers with a pop at the end, focusing anywhere but at the two sitting on the sofa drinking coffee.

I can't hide my smirk when I take in the bright red face of the Archangel.

"Coffee!" Helena b-lines for the kitchen with me hot on her heels. "I need coffee before I deal with anything."

"I wouldn't go that far…" Maddison clamps her mouth shut when I shoot her a glare over my shoulder. "I need more, as well." Lifting herself up, she prances after us.

Helena stops in front of the coffee machine, staring at it longingly. Pressing my chest to her back, I reach over her head to pull two mugs from the cabinets. She shivers visibly, and Raphael's groan makes me smile. That should tell him to keep his righteous, angelic ass away from her.

"You're like a dog pissing on things to mark his territory," Helena mumbles, chuckling.

I can't help but laugh at that. "You're mine." Bending my head, I kiss the skin behind her ear, making her groan and press her ass firmly against my groin. "The sooner he knows that, the better for him. I might let him live."

"Whatever." She elbows me, making me grunt in earnest.

What the fuck? I think.

"You okay?" Maddison sounds concerned, and I realize I must've made a sound at the pain in my sternum.

"Yeah." Playing it off like it wasn't a big deal, I grin. "Just trying to make cupcake here feel better with her mosquito muscles."

"You are hilarious, monster boy!" Snatching the mug from my hand, Helena fills it up and moves to sit on the counter. "So…" She drags the word out before taking a long sip, sighing in bliss as she closes her eyes and swallows. "What's the plan?"

Raphael clears his throat, getting my full attention, and I narrow my gaze at him. Shrugging, he rolls his eyes and looks at Helena. I bristle but bite my tongue. My mission now is to hear what the asshole has to say and get rid of him as fast as possible. He seems a little too attached to her for my liking. Maddison giggles, making me want to throw the mug I'm holding at her. When I look at her, she gives me a shit-eating grin. The longer I glare, the bigger her smile grows. She is enjoying this shit a bit too much.

"My suggestion still stands. I should go to the Sanctuary to check for Hector." Raphael opens his mouth, and just like that, the tightness and dullness return to Helena's green eyes.

Filling my own mug with coffee, I take a sip, buying time

to think of what to say. Pulling the chair next to Helena, I tug her closer, placing her seat between my legs. She murmurs something but doesn't comment or pull away. *Demon one: Angel zero*, I gloat inside, looking pointedly at Raphael. He has the right mind to look ashamed.

"Pay attention, Eric. It's not a pissing contest for a piece of steak." Helena sounds tired, and I feel stupid for acting like an ass. I just can't seem to stop letting the Archangel rub me the wrong way only by being here.

"We can split up. Helena and I can check the Sanctuary while you and Maddison check the laboratory." And just like that, Raphael manages to shoot to the top of my shit list, even rising above Michael.

"Like fuck you'll go anywhere with my mate alone."

"It's just so we don't waste time…" Raphael tries to reason, his eyes pleading with Helena, and I feel rage bubbling like lava inside me.

"Eric…" Helena says, but I'm already up, and my hand is wrapped around Raphael's throat, lifting him off his seat. "Would you please stop!" she pokes me on my shoulder.

I'm beyond hearing or talking. All I want is to separate the Archangels head from his neck. Some metal song starts blaring, making all of us freeze, and Maddison pulls out her phone, glancing at it before she jerks up staring at us wide-eyed. She lifts her phone, pointing the screen at us.

"It's Michael."

Chapter Thirteen

HELENA

"You have Michael's phone number?" I gape at Maddison, stupefied.

"Well, yes." She shifts uncomfortably. "It's not like I didn't try calling him after he took you." She looks insulted, but that didn't even cross my mind. "The phone was off the whole time. I couldn't even trace it."

I don't have time to correct her before Eric releases Raphael, shoving him away like a dirty sock. He snatches the phone from Maddison. Raphael coughs weakly, rubbing his neck, wisely deciding to say nothing.

"What the fuck do you want?" Eric snarls, pressing the phone to his ear.

I'm so pissed off at him acting like a caveman that I want to slap him. Maybe another bullet in his ass will snap him out of it. A girl can dream. I grab the phone from his hand, and pressing the speaker button, hold it between us. He has murder written all over his face, but at my raised eyebrow, he only presses his lips into a thin, white line, his nostrils flaring in anger. Maybe there is hope for him after all.

"Eric, I was hoping you would be the one to answer my call. We need to talk." Michael's voice comes over the speaker, calm and measured, like he didn't play the psycho holding me locked up for two weeks.

"We need to do nothing," Eric snarls again. "I will keep my promise. Next time we cross paths, you will die."

"It might be a little more complicated than you can comprehend." Arrogance is oozing from Michael, making my hand shake where I'm holding the phone suspended between Eric and I.

"You ran out of blood, asshole?" I can't stay quiet anymore. The memories of everything are still fresh in my mind. "Maybe you should come to get it now that we are on more equal ground."

"Ah! Helena. It's good to know you are well." Michael almost sounds relieved I survived, confusing the shit out of me. "I was worried you got damaged in the blast."

"Damaged? I'm not a toy you, asshole! There is something seriously wrong with you, dude." My words are spoken slowly.

Uneasiness is crawling through my insides.

Michael sounds too happy about hearing my voice. That in itself is screaming disaster. Eric is still as a statue, looking at me strangely. Not in the wrong way. The worry I see lurking in his gaze makes me nauseous, however. Raphael perks up at this, sitting straight even as his shoulders stiffen. Maddison is the only one with a calculated look on her face.

"What can we help you with, handsome?" she purrs, winking at me.

As it was expected, the two men in the room look at her as if she's lost her mind. Well, in Eric's case, like he wants to punch her in the face. Nothing new. My mate is taking this whole Michael business personally; not that I blame him. I'd feel the same if he was the one that was taken. Michael speaks again, pulling me out of my thoughts.

"I might've gone about this the wrong way." It sounds like it's painful for the Archangel to admit he might have done something wrong. "I think if we sit and talk about it, you will see the wisdom of my actions." There is a long pause. "We can all get what we want in the end."

"All I have to do is bleed more, huh?" I can't help adding bitterly. And then it hits me. "Where the hell is Hector?"

"What?" Confusion oozes from Michael's voice, and it's too real to be faked.

Maddison groans, covering her face with her hand and telling me without words that I'm an idiot. Raphael shakes his head but still says nothing, like he doesn't want Michael to know that he is here, which makes me more suspicious of him. Eric, on the other hand, hasn't moved a muscle and is still watching me strangely.

"Hector. Where is he?" The cat is already out of the bag, so I just roll with it.

"How should I know where he is? I'm not his shepherd. He has proven where his loyalties are, so I have no time for those like him." Michael sounds almost insulted by the idea of keeping tabs on my father. "We are wasting words. I'm willing to meet."

"How very gracious of you." Sweetness drips from my words like honey, but my mind is spinning, trying to come up with where to begin looking for my father.

I sincerely hoped, if the hand that's still somewhere in this apartment belongs to Hector, that Michael had been the one that sent it. Now that I think about it, it can't possibly be him. He was in ruins from that damn building where he kept me when we left. He didn't have time to send it before we got here. Unless he knew that Eric was going to get me out at that moment. Judging by his anger, and what he said to Raphael, he didn't know. So, that rules him out. My heart picks up a beat with this new development. As messed up as it was, I kind of felt better knowing it was only Michael I had to deal with. Now we know that the bomb that went off was placed by a third party. Someone that was obviously watching from the shadows and had enough time to organize delivery from the time it took us to leave the destroyed building until we got here. Having an unknown adversary added to the disaster that is my life doesn't make me excited about the future.

No, it makes me livid.

"When and where?" We all look at Maddison like we've never seen her before.

I can't believe she is even considering meeting with Michael. I don't need to be a genius to know that the asshole will try to set us up. Eric seems like he is contemplating every way he can kill Maddison, and even though at the moment that might sound like the best idea any of us has had, we must think straight and not turn on each other. Maybe that's the Archangel's plan. Placing my hand on his arm, I turn Eric's attention to me and away from Maddison. If I've learned anything about the too beautiful woman to be anything but a supernatural being, I've learned that she is ahead of the game most of the time. Apart from being blindsided when Michael took me, she always has a plan B, C, and D, followed by the rest of the alphabet. I nod at her in understanding, although Eric still looks ready to kill someone. Not necessarily an Archangel either.

Raphael is shaking his head, showing his reluctance

about meeting his brother while still being quiet, not announcing his presence. Maddison doesn't look like she cares what the Archangel thinks. Instead, she keeps watching me, like my opinion is the one she values. I can almost hear the gears in her brain turning in the silence that surrounds us. I'm too messed up in the head to think straight or make calculated risks. Eric is still teetering on the edge of sanity after I was taken, and it'll be a while before he is back to his old self, looking at the situation objectively. Raphael is the wild card; none of us know exactly where he stands, or what he will actually gain by putting his lot in with the rest of us. That only leaves her.

This is the moment of truth.

Do I trust her enough to let her take control of the situation, or go head-first into deeper shit than I already am? That's when I realize, I do trust her. Me.

A demon hunter, trusting a demon.

I glance at Eric from the corner of my eye. Rephrase that! A demon hunter trusting a demon, and the Prince of Hell. Well, my life took a nose-dive, didn't it?

"You name the place and time." Michael shocks all of us. "I'll be there."

Chapter Fourteen

HELENA

"We need time to think. I will call you back." Reaching her hand forward, Maddison hangs up on Michael without giving him a chance to say anything else. I'm still holding the phone between Eric and me.

Raphael and Eric jump for the throat at the same time, rounding on Maddison. Raphael yelling while cussing is predominant in Eric's shouts. She just sits back in her chair, calmly watching them. Following her example, I pull out a chair and plop into it with a sigh.

Apparently, it's too much to ask for a little time to regroup without drama around these guys. They all have a short fuse, except Maddison. The urgency that was gnawing at me about Hector to find him, and make sure he kept breathing, was still pressing on my mind. But, somewhere in the back of my mind, I was hoping I'd do it at my pace. Take a breather first, I guess.

That was not written in the stars for me.

Wrapping my cold fingers around the coffee mug, taking a long sip, I watch dispassionately as the angel and the demon keep snarling at Maddison, wildly waving their arms and shaking their fists. Their words are like an annoying buzzing of a mosquito in the middle of the night around me. I ignore both of them, not taking my eyes away from Maddison. She is doing the same, her gaze focused on me intently.

Something changed.

In the few minutes between that phone ringing and the time she hung up on the Archangel, something shifted between us. It hangs like a palpable thing in the kitchen, thickening the air around us like molasses. A distant beat starts in my chest, separate from my heartbeat, like another being is residing inside my body. The longer I'm focused on her, the stronger the beat makes itself known. Like a war drum. I can feel it pulsing, and I'm unable to do anything else but keep looking at her. Panic is building, my mind screaming that something is wrong with me, yet I sit as calm as a rabbit snarled in the gaze of a wolf.

A violent shiver shakes me to my core, my body visibly shivering like I'm sitting in my bikini outside in the middle of the winter in Alaska. I grind my teeth, clutching the mug, sloshing hot coffee over my wrists, unable to pull away from Maddison's hypnotizing gaze. My body keeps shaking, stronger with each breath I take, and I realize I'm panting.

Maddison blinks, releasing me from whatever stare-down we had happening between us.

My eyes dart towards Eric, confusion clouding my thoughts at the openmouthed look he is giving me. Glancing at Raphael doesn't help. The distressed look on the Archangel's face is like a punch to the stomach. That's when I realize that they are trying to balance so they can keep standing, and it's not me shivering. Maddison is clutching the counter in a white-knuckled grip, not moving from her seat. The entire building is shaking like it has been hit by an earthquake that is getting stronger by the second.

"Hel." Eric lifts his hand, reaching hesitantly towards my face. I didn't mean to flinch, and the hurt flashing in his green eyes is like a hot poker to my chest. "Calm down, beautiful. Breathe." Dropping his hand limply to his side, he clenches his fist.

"I don't think we have time for her to breathe." Maddison snaps at him. "Helena, pull your shit together or you'll bring the entire building down on our heads. Think of the humans that will die. We will survive."

The shaking abruptly stops.

I feel like a bucket of cold water was dumped on my head. My heart is trying to beat its way out of my chest, and I look from one person to the next in panic, hoping they'll tell me what the hell is going on. *I did that? How?* My mind is spinning like a tornado, making me feel dizzy.

"See?" Maddison gloats, staring down her nose at Eric." That's how you deal with a woman."

"What is going on?" My voice sounds faint, breathless.

"I think you got a little riled up," Maddison chirps, as if my emotions causing a skyscraper to shake is an everyday occurrence.

Opening my mouth and pointedly ignoring her, I turn to Eric, but he is not looking at me. Coiled up like a snake, he is glaring venom at the Archangel. Afraid of what I'll see, I slowly and hesitantly turn to look at Raphael. His yellow eyes are watching me intently, and if I didn't know better, I would think he is expecting something else from me. To grow another head maybe? At my raised eyebrow, he snaps out of it, shrugging his shoulder in answer to my unspoken question.

Eric loses his shit.

One second, he is glaring daggers, with me sitting between Raphael and him. The next, he has the Archangel up by the neck, dangling him like a dog with a chew toy. Me and Maddison both jump up, ready to intervene and stop Eric from killing Raphael, when he hisses at us like some angry cat, freezing us in place. Shadows spread from the corners of the kitchen, an ominous feeling saturating the very air I'm breathing.

"What the fuck did you two do to her!" he roars, shaking Raphael menacingly.

It's an impressive display of strength because Raphael is as tall as Eric and just as packed with muscle. Seeing them like this, you'd think the Archangel doesn't weigh more than a couple of pounds, his feet kicking off the ground. His face is reddening; finally, his long fingers wrap around Eric's wrist, trying to dislodge him. For some reason, this whole situation doesn't horrify me. Leaning my hip on the chair, crossing my hands over my chest and tilting my head, I wait to see what happens.

Eric has every right to be angry. I should be more furious, although at the moment I'm still shaken up from what happened. I wasn't able to do this until now, and God knows I've been angry before. More times than I can count. Something in me has changed in the time I was held captive, and just like Eric, I want to know what that is.

"He has a point, Raphael." The look of betrayal in the Archangels eyes doesn't bother me as much as it should.

Maybe Michael did break me. I know that Raphael won't die from lack of air. It's not like I've seen someone choke an angel in front of me until now, but I know this to be true, deep to my soul. None of these supernatural beings need to do anything the rest of us humans do to stay alive. They mimic it perfectly, blending in like a snake in the grass, but they don't need it. Why I'm so sure about my observation, I have no clue, yet, I don't move to stop Eric. Seeing there will be no help coming from me, Raphael's hands begin glowing that green light I saw when he healed me, and Eric dropped him, hissing in pain.

The Archangel makes a show of slowly straightening up his shirt, smoothing his hair with both hands, blowing out a deep breath. The silence in the room is almost choking me, but I refuse to let it show, or move my eyes away from them.

"Well?" Sounding bored, I watch him expectantly.

"It's nothing bad..." Raphael trails off when Eric bursts, spitting profanities at him.

Even my ears blush from some of them. Apparently, my mate gets very creative when pissed off. Good to know. Wanting to hear the explanation, I push myself off the chair and walk up to Eric. His yelling stops immediately, his amber gaze locking on me in an instant. My lips twitch at the corners, but I force myself not to smile. He looks breathtaking, being all protective of me. That's another indication that I'm broken if I find that acceptable.

"We need to let him speak, or we won't know what was done to me." As soon as my arm goes halfway around his back, he tucks me under his shoulder, angling his body in a protective stance between Raphael and me.

"Nothing was done to you, Helena." Raphael sounds insulted.

"Speak!" Eric snarls, while I glance at Maddison since she's uncharacteristically quiet.

She is watching things unfold with a calculated look, and I have a nagging feeling that she is seeing more than any of us in the whole situation. Her eyes twinkle with excitement when they lock on mine. It happens so fast that I'm sure I've imagined it.

"Nothing was done to hurt her, Eric!" Raphael snarls angrily, surprising me so much that I jerk in Eric's arms. "Nothing on my part," he amends, a guilty look crossing over his face.

"Time is wasting, as the Holy ass would say," I remind him, getting a surprised chuckle from Maddison.

"You are part angel, part demon." Raphael tries hard not to smile at my jab, but his lips lift slightly at the corners nonetheless. He is waiting, so I nod in acknowledgment. "When you were too weak after Michael visited your room…"

Eric goes stiff as a surfboard, and my glare cuts Raphael off. Clearing my throat, I'm doing my best to relay a message without saying a word that he needs to skip that part, or I have a feeling next time Eric snaps nothing will hold him back from ripping the Archangel limb from limb.

"I'm trying to say that I've healed you a dozen times," Raphael continues, unaware that those words don't help either. "Every time after the first one, you actually absorbed the energy, rather than me pushing it towards you." Tilting his head, Raphael gives me a once over. "Almost as if I was feeding you."

"I will feed you to the vermin in a second if you don't get to the point," Eric tells him through clenched teeth. For some stupid reason, I grin like an idiot, making Raphael frown at me.

"My theory, if you will"—squaring his shoulders, Raphael pulls on the sleeves of his shirt—"is that, because of her unique makeup, the characteristics from either of the sides get stronger the more time she spends around either of us. Angel, or demon. Or if there is an energy exchange." The pointed look he gives me shouts "I know what you did this morning," but I ignore him, my mind doing gymnastics after the information he so nonchalantly gave us.

"You're trying to say if I spend time with you, I'll eventually turn into an angel, or if I spend time with Eric, I'll turn into a demon?" The thought is really troubling, subconsciously making me glance at Eric from the corner of my eye.

"He doesn't know what the fuck he is talking about," Eric spits angrily.

"Your jealousy will cost her greatly in the long run, Eric." Raphael loses his cool, glaring. "I'm not trying to take her from you." The snort coming from Eric at those words sounds so arrogant I punch him in the ribs, making him grunt in pain. Raphael smiles like he has seen his newborn for the first time, pissing me off.

"I'll ask again. Why are you helping me?" Lifting a hand, I shut him up from giving me bullshit. "The real reason Raphael, or get the hell out."

"I knew your mother." I feel like he sucker-punched me in the stomach at those words. "I couldn't save her, but I can help you."

Chapter Fifteen

ERIC

If I ever learned anything in my long life, it's that the shiny fuckers who think they are too good for the rest of us love dropping bombs at the most inappropriate times. Just like what Raphael did with his statement. Glancing at Helena proves it when I see she's too shocked to do anything but stare incredulously at him.

"You knew my mother?" There is so much hope and pain in her whispered question, I'm debating how long it'll take her to forgive me if I just kill him.

Raphael ignores my glare pointedly, clearing his throat. "Yes, I knew her. And I think who she and your father were is what makes you so unique. You see, she was an angel of mercy." He takes a long pause, maybe expecting a reaction from Helena, but she only stares at him unblinking. "Your father was a demon of vengeance. Two different powers, yet they worked perfectly together as a team. A Yin and a Yang. In the end, it didn't matter what they meant to each other because all the fighting to stay together was for nothing. Or so I thought, until we found you. I wasn't planning on bringing this up, but seeing what kind of predicament I find myself in…"

I exchange a meaningful look with Maddison. She is watching the Archangel as well, her narrowed gaze telling me she smells bullshit. I wisely keep my mouth shut. Helena is frustrated by my behavior as is, so no need to push my luck any further.

"Before we get into that hornets' nest…" Shaking her head, she pulls herself out of the shock Raphael gave her, making my chest puff up with pride. "What did you do to me?" The wary look she gives me when she glances at me slays me. "How much did you change me?"

"I didn't change you!" Raphael stutters defensively, which causes my fists to clench. "It's who you are. My energy when I was healing you only brought it to the surface. It would've manifested eventually anyway." No matter his calm demeanor, he can't hide the uncertainty lurking in his eyes.

"Right," Helena drawls. "You just sped up the process."

"You could say that," Raphael mumbles hesitantly.

For some reason, thoughts of Abaddon assault my mind out of nowhere. Shaking my head like I can physically make them go away, I grab my mug of coffee and gulp it down in two swallows. I know if I stay here, I won't be able to stop myself from at least hurting the Archangel. Thinking all I needed to do was find Helena, and everything would be right again was a really short sighted thing to do. In my anger, I didn't care about anything else. Now, here I am without any information about what's going on around us. I need to check my channels and see if we can get the upper hand. Helena put a bullet between Abaddon's eyes, sending him back to Hell when he helped Michael ambush us that night. From everything I know about the slimy weasel, he will be back before we know it. If he felt slighted by her actions, he might be behind this mess with Hector. Not wanting to give her false hope so I can only fail her, I don't share my thoughts on that.

"I will be back." Releasing Helena after kissing her temple, I head out like the hounds of Hell are on my heels.

"Wanna share with the rest of the class what got into you?" Helena calls after me. Maddison's chuckle grinds on my nerves.

"I will check the word on the streets about our situation." Turning around, walking backward, I give her a reassuring smile. "I think Raphael will tell you more if I'm not around. Things he is trying not to say in front of me. He is not wrong in thinking I'll pluck his wings one feather at a time." Grinning, my gaze locks on his, telling him I'm only calm because I don't want to upset my mate. "I can always do that later." With a wink, I leave the apartment and my frowning mate.

Jumping in the SUV Maddison had left in front of the building last night, I drive aimlessly around the city. Taking back roads, unwilling to get stuck in city traffic in downtown Atlanta, my mind goes over everything I know so far. The bomb was not placed as a precaution against me. I was hoping Michael expected me to catch up to him eventually, so he had it as a backup. The bastard didn't know it was there. Neither did Raphael, or he wouldn't have taken Helena through that exit. What his motives are is irrelevant right now. As much as it pisses me off to have him around her, begrudgingly, I admit he helped me find her. Not knowing his agenda is leaving me uneasy. For now, I have to let it play out. Too many unknowns are involved for my liking, and I can use all the help I can get to keep my mate safe. I'm not too proud to accept the said help from an angel. I might not like it, but I'll take what I can get.

In my musings, I realize that I've driven to the same bar where Helena and I met up with Abaddon. Maybe thinking about him and that night subconsciously brought me here. Checking around for unseen threats, I park in the empty parking lot. Leaning my forearms on the steering wheel, tilting my face on them, I take everything in. The building looks long forgotten, like no one has been here since that night. If my eyes are not deceiving me, even the blood from Abaddon is still a dark stain on the dirt close to the doors.

Abaddon has always been an ambitious fucker, but that night, he overreached his potential. Siding with the Archangel, against Maddison and me. I would've believed anything possible but that. He is not a demon overly concerned about others unless there is something in it for him. But what could he possibly want from an Archangel? He couldn't have been so stupid to think that anyone from Heaven's squad would help him in any way. Whatever his reasons, he stood on the wrong side of the fence that night. I shouldn't be wasting my time here; memories of things past don't help anyone. Annoyed with my own racing mind, slamming both hands on the steering wheel in frustration, I turn on the engine.

The day is gray and cloudy, humidity clinging to the shiny paint of the vehicle like drops of rain. Spinning around and ready to hit the gas pedal to get out of the place, I blink a couple of times at the outline of a man leaning heavily on the side of the building. My mind says a drunk or a homeless person, but at a second glance, those clothes are recognizable anywhere.

A hunter.

Slamming on the breaks, I'm out of the SUV faster than

the time the engine needs to cut off after I press the button. The man is pinned by his throat on the side of the building, his feet kicking the air between us.

"Wrong day to pick me as your target, little human." Snarling in his face, I bare my teeth.

Gasping, he claws at my hand that is wrapped around his throat. It's pathetic; his attempts at fighting me are severely lacking. Pushing myself out of his face and preparing the snap, his neck is not as satisfying as I would like it to be. His gasping words save his life.

"Helena…" he rasps, freezing me in place.

"What did you say?" My words and the malice in my voice give even me chills.

He keeps clawing at my hand, his face turning purple. I release him, dropping him at my feet like the scum that he is. The Order tried to hurt mine and my mate. I should kill them all one by one. He coughs weakly, sputtering a prayer and making me bristle.

"Your God will not help you here, human. You have exactly one second to speak." He shivers violently, hearing my voice that's more demon than human at the moment.

"Helena." Lifting his head up, his gaze filled with terror, he swallows thickly. "I must speak to Helena, please."

"And who the fuck are you?" Letting the amber glow fill my eyes, I smile when he flinches.

"Jared." Lifting his chin in the first sign of defiance, he locks his blue gaze with mine. "I'm part of her team!"

Chapter Sixteen

HELENA

Watching the door close behind Eric, leaves me conflicted. The three of us stay quiet for a while, uncomfortable silence rubbing me wrong like a pair of unbroken-in shoes. Was it my curiosity about Raphael's allegations that drove Eric to flee like the building was on fire? After hearing that the Archangel brought some angelic traits out in me, did he regret searching for me? Mate or not, he is the son of Lucifer. If I'm more angel than demon, aren't I against everything he stands for?

An ungraceful snort escapes me. Shaking my head, I turn away from Maddison and Raphael's questioning looks, staring out the window. My vision turns unfocused when the memory of the night I met the Archangel Michael for the first time pulls me from reality. His words echo in my head.

"Your mother was an angel," Michael cuts off my tirade, and I close my mouth.

"Is she...alive?" I hate that my voice breaks, so I clear my throat. "Is she still alive?"

"No, she is not." Hector is the one that speaks, and I slowly turn towards him, searching his eyes.

"Neither your mother nor your father is alive, Helena." Unshed tears glisten in his eyes, but they turn cold when he looks at Michael. "You better tell her everything, since you started this!"

"What more can there be?" I look from one to the other. "My mother was an angel, my father, human..." My words trail off when Hector winces. "What?" Snapping the word out, I wave the guns again.

"Your father was a demon." Michael's emotionless voice is like a punch to my solar plexus.

"No!" My scream echoes around the library, bouncing off the walls and sounding like multiple people screaming at once. Fear and anger mixed together in a cocktail of such intense emotions that I feel like I might burst into pieces where I stand. "You're lying! I'm not an abomination!"

"You're not, Hel!" Hector tries to comfort me, and the asshole angel snorts at my nickname. I glare at him. "No matter what anyone says, you are not an abomination, and no one doubts your loyalty."

"Could've fooled me!" Still glaring at Michael, I start taking slow steps back again. "So, what does this mean?" Alarms are blaring in my head, the gut feeling in my GPS redoubles and I can't ignore it anymore. There is definitely something evil here, but how is that possible? Or...am I the evil? The thought almost makes me double over, but I force myself to keep slowly moving away from them. "Am I evil? Is that why you're here?"

"You are not evil..."

"The demon that scratched you took your blood with him to Hell. They know who and what you are now, and they need your blood to keep the gate open. I cannot let that happen." Michael straightens up, and for the first time, fear grips me like hands squeezing my throat.

He is not a demon or a normal human that I can just fight off. Blessed metal, salt, and Holy water won't do him harm. No matter *how strong I am, there is no way I can fight him and win. So how in the hell am I going to protect myself from him? At the moment, he looks exactly like what he is, a warrior Archangel. His blue eyes are shimmering like liquid silver and his blinding white wings with golden tips spread out around him as he takes a step towards me. Hector screams like a banshee and throws himself at Michael, but the angel only pushes him away one-handed, like he's flicking off lint from his shirt.*

"You cannot win this fight, Helena. I should've done this the day we found you, but Raphael is sometimes too sentimental for his own good. I cannot allow you to live. We all must sacrifice for the greater good of all."

"Helena?" Raphael's voice brings me back to the present.

Blinking a couple of times to clear my vision, I turn back to where he and Maddison are still sitting at the kitchen counter. Both of them have concerned looks on their faces, watching me as if expecting me to lose my shit at any moment. They are not far from the truth. My breathing is haggard, hands clammy from cold sweat that's drenching my body, while anxiety eats a hole inside my chest.

"I'm fine."

Blowing out a deep breath, I walk back to my chair. The scraping sound it makes when I twist it around to sit has both of them flinching. Supernatural hearing is not always a plus, I guess. My movement slows down, that thought freezing me in the air right before my butt connects with the leather of the chair.

"Unless you want me to start freaking out, I need you to tell me what's wrong." Maddison snaps her fingers a couple of times in front of my face. "You look like you've seen a ghost."

"How much exactly did you change me, Raphael?" Ignoring Maddison, I watch the Archangel like a hawk.

His eyebrows jerk up in surprise, but he schools his features from one blink to the next. The calm mask slides into place so fast that if I weren't watching him so intently, I would've missed it. The yellow glow of his angelic eyes pulses once as if in warning, lodging a lump the size of my fist in my throat.

"I'll repeat it, Helena. I did not change you." The tone of his voice can put a feral beast into a peaceful sleep. "I only tried to help you, but I did notice a slight change in you after I did that."

"And you didn't think it was important to let me know, right?" Tilting my head, I watch for any other signs that he is not telling the whole truth.

"There was nothing to tell." A line forms above the bridge of his nose, disturbing the perfect features on his face. "You are a good person, Helena. Having angelic traits is not a bad thing."

"Being a good person does not make me an angel, Raphael." Hissing at him through clenched teeth, I do my best to calm my temper. The assholes think they can do whatever they like with the rest of us and we should wag our tails like good little pets at their mercy. "Just like sinning does not make me a demon. You had no right to keep it from me." My whole body is trembling in anger.

"Helena snap out of it!" Maddison grabs my forearm, shaking me out of the red haze that started clouding my vision.

Oh, crap!

The building is shaking again, but it isn't my body trembling. Groaning and rubbing my hands over my face, I'm taking slow, deep breaths to calm down. Gradually, my mind clears and I can think reasonably again, my heart slowing down the relentless beat against my breastbone.

"You are neither of those things, Helena. You are… other." Reaching his hand as if he was thinking of touching me, Raphael snatches it back when a menacing growl raises the hairs on the back of my neck.

Checking over my shoulder, I expected to see Eric back. Not seeing anyone, I slowly turn my head, looking from Maddison to Raphael. The beautiful redhead is grinning proudly, like a parent at their child's first stage performance. The Archangel looks disturbed and constipated, his eyes rounded and too big for his face. A sinking feeling tells me the terrifying sound came from me. Raphael's comment about the exchange of energy hit home finally. Hysterical laughter bursts from me and tears stream down my face. I laugh for a long time, slapping my hand on the kitchen counter. When I finally get myself under control, I notice both of them watching me like I have finally lost my mind. And maybe I have. At the moment, everything is so messed up and ridiculous, I don't even care.

"Other, indeed, Archangel." Still chuckling and shaking my head, I stand up and walk away, leaving them murmuring softly behind me. "Other, indeed…"

Chapter Seventeen

ERIC

"She doesn't have a team, human." Grabbing a handful of his shirt, I lift the hunter up and slam his back against the wall. "Did you forget all of you tried to kill her? Or did the Order give you some happy juice to wash out your brain?"

"She will always have a team!" The human finds his courage whenever his team is mentioned. It's almost adorable how he glares at me one moment and cowers the next. "We didn't try to hurt her. We've been doing our best to help her as much as we can."

"Is that so?"

"Yes! And if you ask her, you will know I'm telling the truth." Seeing my clenched fist lift in the air, Jared stumbles over his own words. "Call her and ask her! Just tell her...just say you found Jared, and you'll see. She won't be happy if you hurt me." Gulping, he clumps his mouth shut with an audible click.

He just said the only thing that can actually save him. Helena won't be happy. My mate cares too much about people, even those that have done nothing but hurt her.

Hearing Raphael say her mother was an angel of mercy rings true in my soul. The woman has a heart bigger than this realm. It might be her downfall, but I admire that about her. Even when it pisses me off. Maybe it's a bad idea to hurt the hunter, but I can still toss him around a little. Just to make sure he thinks twice if he ever considers crossing her.

Lifting him off the ground, I throw him a few feet away, the dust from the dried-up soil puffing up a cloud around him. With slow, measured steps, I stalk him, one corner of my mouth lifted in a wicked smile. His eyes widen comically, and he blanches, scrambling to get his feet under him, like a turtle trying to right itself after being flipped upside down.

"Where is Hector?" Letting my fingers change to claws, I watch him sputter, almost swallowing his own tongue. "Speak now or you may never say another word."

"That's why I need to speak to her." After a coughing fit, his hands waving away the cloud of dust still hanging around him, Jared clears his throat. "We saw that you took her away from that historical building where Archangel Michael kept her. You beat us to it by a day. We had everything planned to get her out." Shaking his head sadly, he almost looks regretful that I saved my mate. "Hector disappeared a couple of days after Helena was taken by Michael. No one has seen him since."

I stop advancing, watching his eyes dart around searching for a way out, or maybe expecting help? Nostrils flaring, filling my lungs with the dusty air, I can't sense anyone else around us. Not for a mile or so at least. So, I wait. When he doesn't get any response from me, Jared huffs out a heavy breath.

"We didn't see him or hear from him at all, so we concentrated on finding and helping Hel." Glancing uneasily at me, he looks at my nose, not meeting my eyes.

"That was until two days ago when we accidentally over-heard two of our patrons mention his name."

"Saying what exactly?" Unable to stop myself, I growl the words at him.

He jerks like he has been punched, a shudder visibly shaking his body. I've forgotten how jumpy the hunters are when faced with one of us. As if breathing the same air will make them catch a demon disease. Snorting at my own joke, I grin menacingly at him.

"They mentioned that no matter what was done to him, he will help them get their hands on Helena. I was keeping watch so we are not seen listening to something that might get us killed. I didn't hear all of it. From what George said after, they were planning to take Helena even from the Archangel. They had plans for her that made George act insane for hours. If you know him, you'll know that's saying a lot."

The name George nudges my brain like an insistent poker. I've heard it before. And then it hits me, the night at this very place, the hunter that I didn't think survived. Helena's friend. The one that helped me get her out of here and away from Michael's clutches, at least for the time being. Maybe the guy is not full of shit and only trying to save his skin. I pay closer attention to him. There are beads of sweat gathered along his hairline and on his upper lip. He is terrified of me; there is no question about it. But he is not trying to run away like any sane human will do. His hands are shaking, even when he clenches his fists in a futile attempt to hide it, yet he stands in front of me, doing his best to convince me to let him see my mate. I'm not sure if it's the mention of George or the other things I started noticing about him, but I decide to take him with me. Hunter or not, if he even breathes wrong in Helena's direction, I'll kill him before he can blink. She will have to forgive me for it, no matter how long it takes.

"You speak the truth." Rolling my shoulders, I crack my neck to release the tension.

"I might not be the brightest bulb in the box, but I'm not stupid," he says, so matter-a-fact, I burst out laughing.

"That remains to be seen, human. Let us not jump to conclusions, huh?" My claws retract, Jared visibly relaxing at that.

"I really thought you'd kill me before I got a chance to explain why I followed you." Chuckling uneasily, he wipes his forehead and upper lip with the back of his hand. "I can honestly say I haven't been this scared in my life."

"Good." His head snaps up at my words. Waving my hand to put him at ease, I shrug my shoulder. "If you are not scared of me, you have no self-preservation. Hunter or not, you're still human. Fighting rogues is one thing. Facing something like me is an entirely different story."

"So, it's true then? You really are..." he cuts himself off abruptly, pressing his lips in a thin line to physically stop himself from speaking.

"A demon?" Cocking my head to the side, I smirk at him.

"The Prince of Hell." Gulping, thinking I can't hear him, he mumbles, "God help me."

Throwing my head back, I laugh from the bottom of my being. Slapping my hand on my thigh, wiping tears from my eyes, I can't help but walk up to him. He flinches but doesn't pull away when I grab his shoulder, turning him around to walk towards the SUV. Dragging his feet only slightly, he follows, his body rigid.

"I think I might like you, Jared." His reaction to my statement is more violent than when I was advancing on him to separate his head from his body. He stumbles and twitches, like I've punched him.

"Tha..." he squeaks before clearing his throat. "Thank you."

"Me liking you might not be a good thing." I bare my teeth at him. "It all depends on what Helena says. I can like you and still think of many creative ways to end your miserable life. You better start praying to your God that you're not plotting against my mate."

"I would never hurt Hel. I would be dead many times over if not for her having my back. I don't care if I die, as long as I can help her and repay some of it." For the first time, he looks unafraid, squaring his shoulders.

Slapping him on the back, making him stumble a couple of steps, I open the passenger door. "Get your ass inside. You might live a lot longer than you hoped for if that is the case."

Leaving him gaping at me, I jog around the vehicle. I should've known the Order would not stay out of this. For all their righteousness, there are some greedy fuckers for power, even in those waving the cross in the faces of the rest of us. I just hope Helena takes the unfortunate news well.

Chapter Eighteen

HELENA

The unsettling feeling after Eric left so suddenly slowly fades away, and I realize that I'm grateful that he left. I need some time away from everyone so I can think. Closing the bedroom door softly behind me, I kick my boots off one by one. I'm going to use the tub that resembles a small pool for the first time. Nothing can calm your mind like water. Placing my guns gently on the tallboy, I stare at them for a moment. Ever since I held them in my hands, they felt like a part of me. After being away for two weeks, they feel foreign and strange. Like the bond I had with them is broken. Or maybe I'm the one broken. Whatever it is, all I can do is trace every line on the metal with detachment.

Lifting a hand, my fingers trace the barrel with a featherlight touch. The calmness I always felt when my skin would glide over them is not there. Have I really changed that much? More importantly, did Raphael change me that much with whatever he did? Just like everything in my life nowadays, I have too many questions and not enough answers. Blowing out a slow breath, I turn away from my guns and drop my clothing whichever way they fall on my way to the bathroom.

Passing the mirror makes me stop and slowly turn to look at my reflection, naked as the day I was born. The dark circles under my eyes are almost gone, and my skin is looking healthy. Glancing down, I twist my arms this way and that, frowning in confusion. The bruises that felt like permanent markings for almost two weeks are gone. Clear, smooth skin meets my gaze in the mirror. Did Eric heal them? I sure couldn't, because they would've been gone before I got out of that place if that was the case. Another question without an answer.

I push that to the back of my mind, along with everything else I can't figure out. Lo and behold, the queen of suppressing emotions. Turning my focus to the flat surface of the water, I lower my body in it. Warmth envelops me, instantly making all the tension slowly fade away. With a deep sigh, I lean my back against the warm tiles, tilting my head back and closing my eyes. The quiet around me is a welcomed companion. After being alone for most of the time I was kept locked up, I thought I'd never want to be alone again if I ever got out of there. I was wrong. There is wisdom in silence, I just never knew to appreciate it until now. With my body feeling lighter and the water carrying my weight like an embrace, I gradually drift away. I don't fight it. Thoughts of my real parents try to push to the forefront of my mind, but I fight against it tooth and nail. Anything is better than overthinking at the moment.

Something jerks me out of my light sleep. I wasn't really sleeping, more like a meditative state where you drift off, yet you're aware of every sound and shift around you. Not opening my eyes, I stay still, straining my ears to hear whatever it is that brought me back to reality. That's when I realize it isn't a sound that woke me up.

It is a presence.

The energy that radiates in the bathroom pebbles my skin with its power. How I've never noticed this until this very moment is beyond me. The intensity, the pull I feel at the center of my chest, the way my heartbeat instantly syncs in with his. If I could've denied my bond with Eric until this very moment, it all goes down the drain right now. There is no mistaking that my soul is connected with his. But, is it by fate, or by our own making?

I feel the stirring of the air, although he is as silent as a ghost on his feet. The closer he gets to me, the stronger my reaction is to him, like my body is trying to scream at me for daring to ignore him and not acknowledging his presence. Even with my eyes closed, I can feel his gaze marking every line, dip, and curve of my body. His intent focus is like a physical touch making my breathing speed up.

"I wasn't sure if you heard me come in." His words are soft, the deep timbre of his voice making me shiver.

My lips curve into a smile when I turn my face towards the sound of his voice, still not opening my eyes. "I didn't." For whatever reason, my answer is just as soft, as if we don't want to disturb the silence. "I felt you, however."

"Is this one of the new developments?" Eric sounds hesitant, making me finally look at him.

He is leaning against the wall, his arms folded over his chest and one leg crossed over the other at the ankles. One foot is resting on the tip of his shitkickers while his gaze is focused on my face. My smile grows at how careful he is to not let his eyes wander, thinking it will upset me at the moment. For all the noise he likes to make and his bad boy attitude, demon boy, is very considerate. Almost sweet, but I wouldn't dare tell him that. After the scare I gave him when Michael snatched me, I'm not sure he would appreciate me taking a jab at his tough, macho ego.

"Maybe...I'm not sure." Barely moving, I shrug a shoulder.

"Why do I feel like I'm not going to like whatever it is that made that smile grow?" Slightly narrowing his eyes, he mockingly glares at me.

"Wouldn't you like to know." Laughing, I wiggle my eyebrows at him.

He peels off the wall, coming to crouch next to my head. "I love it when you laugh, Hel." His warm lips press on my forehead, and my eyelids flutter shut at the contact.

"Yeah, I haven't done much of that lately." Mumbling, I savor the moment.

"If it's up to me, that is all you'll be doing." Pulling away, he searches my eyes.

A lump forms in my throat, and I have to swallow a couple of times to dislodge it. "You'll think I'm a lunatic if I walk around laughing 24/7, Eric."

"Better you be a lunatic than to watch you be sad. When I see that dull look in your eyes, it kills something inside me. It makes me want to kill everything around me to never see it there."

"I'll be fine, I promise. I just need time." Lifting a hand out of the water, I cup his face, and he doesn't even flinch at the rivulets running down his skin. "It wasn't as bad as it could've been. You need to know that." At his incredulous look, I make sure he sees that I'm not saying things to only make him feel better. "I mean it. Did he hurt me? Yes, many times. But"—Raising my voice stops the menacing growl coming from his chest— "that was only because I was fighting him, not letting him draw blood. He always ended up with a few vials but never without paying for it one way or another. I need you to know I gave as much as I got. Unfortunately, he is stronger than me. But I made him bleed, many times."

"That's my girl!" Forcing a smile for my sake, he nuzzles my hand. "Did Raphael tell you anything useful while I was gone?"

"Apart from telling me I'm something 'other' you mean?" Chuckling at Eric's glower, I shake my head. "No, I left them with Maddison because I started shaking the building again. I needed to calm down. I'm sure he will spill the beans. He just needs a nudge. Let me get dressed and we can press him on it."

"That might need to wait a bit." Helping me get out of the pool, Eric wraps me in a towel, pulling me into his arms.

"What do you mean? Did you find out something?" His face is closed off, not letting me know anything.

"I hope you won't get more upset, but I brought a friend of yours back with me."

"What? Who is it?" Pushing out of his arms, I hurry to get dressed.

"He said his name is Jared." My gasp makes Eric nod as if I gave him the confirmation he is searching for. "He was scared shitless of me, but I recognized that same pride you have for your team. Every time he mentioned the rest of his team, he looked a lot less like a little mouse." Chuckling, he twists around, escaping my punch. "I'm joking, Hel. I just want to break the tension..." Snatching me by the arm, he pulls me to him. "I want you to smile now because I'm pretty sure we won't like whatever it is that he wants to tell us."

Chapter Nineteen

ERIC

Walking behind Helena, we enter the living room where Maddison and Raphael are sitting with Jared. I can tell by the way Maddison is sitting on the edge of the sofa that she is forcing herself to engage in small talk, waiting for all of us to be present before hearing what made the hunter seek me out. I was impatient as well on our drive here, wanting to know it all, yet dreading it as well. Humans are capable of unspeakable things in the name of their belief. They have twisted their faith in their maker, believing they are doing the right thing by shunning the sinners, not realizing the shadow slowly creeping up their soul until it's too late. They learn the lesson the hard way when faced with my father. But that's a mess I'll leave to ponder another day.

When Jared sees Helena, whatever he is saying is forgotten. Jumping up from where he is seated, he darts forward and throws his arms around her. Stopping in my tracks, I watch him closely, noticing there is nothing possessive or sexual in his movements. The way he is checking her over, holding her at arm's length, speaks more of family, rather than a love interest. Seeing this makes me relax my body, my coiled muscles unclenching.

"Thank God you are okay, Hel," Jared breathes, tears shimmering in his eyes. "I had to see you for myself to be sure." Glancing my way, hoping I won't notice, he flinches when he sees me watching him. "Not that I doubted that he would get you out of there," Tilting his chin in my direction, he makes Helena look at me over her shoulder, smiling. "I just needed to see you for my own piece of mind."

"Thanks, Jared." Squeezing his arm reassuringly, Helena blows out a long breath. "As much as I would love for us to sit and talk about what happened, that's all in the past, and it can wait. We have pressing matters at the moment. I'm perfectly fine, but I'm not sure the same goes for Hector. Eric said you have information for us."

"We, George, Cass, and I, have been lurking around the Sanctuary ever since you left that night. Things have changed. A lot. I'm not even sure that words can explain the extent of it. We've been feeling like we are living in a twilight zone."

Helena frowns, her fingers twitching like she is missing the weight of her guns at hearing those words. That's when I notice, she doesn't have her weapons on her. Glancing at Maddison, I see her following my line of sight before her eyes jerk back up to my face. Her eyebrows climb up her forehead when she finally understands my confusion, but I shake my head slightly, making sure she understands to keep her mouth shut. There is time to worry about things like that later. We have more significant problems now, as Helena said earlier.

"Changed how? And why aren't the others with you?" Helena is sitting close to Jared as he talks, but she turns towards me and motions me to sit next to her. Smiling like an idiot, I comply straight away. She has me wrapped around her little finger, and the funny thing is, it doesn't bother me at all.

Maddison smirks.

"We're being watched, Hel. I'm sure they expect us to lead you right into their hands. So, we started getting creative, deceiving them into thinking we are inside the Sanctuary while sneaking around. Unfortunately, one or two of us have to be physically seen most of the time so they don't get suspicious."

"You keep saying 'they.' Who are 'they'? Everything you've said so far sounds so ominous, but we are talking about the Sanctuary." Helena rests her hand on my thigh, not looking my way. It doesn't go unnoticed by Jared, his eyes flicking to her hand for a second. It doesn't go unnoticed by Raphael either, the fucker is frowning, making me bare my teeth at him.

"The patrons, Hel. They are locked up in the library day and night, and hunters keep going missing by the dozen. What's worse is that there haven't been any hunts set up or any information of demon nests." Glancing uneasily at me, Jared clears his throat.

"Tell her everything and tell her the truth. Don't worry about insulting me. You won't. We need to know what's going on." Hoping I'll put him at ease, I try smiling reassuringly. That only makes him stiffen and ready to bolt. I frown at his reaction.

"Don't mind Eric. He is harmless." Helena waves a hand in Jared's face. Raphael's eyes almost roll out of his head, and I bite my lip, tasting blood just so I don't laugh. Maddison chokes at those words but covers it with a cough. "Why would the patrons harm any of us? Well, anyone apart from me, since I'm an abomination, or whatever. That doesn't make any sense."

"The reason I came searching for Eric was that we overheard a conversation between Samuel and Adam. They talked about using Hector to get their hands on you, saying that you are a foolish, sentimental girl that will give your life for someone like him. Someone who turned their back on an Archangel to protect a creature that needed to be put down for the sake of humanity. Devil spawn is what they call you." Jared looks ready to cry at that, but Helena listens without any emotion showing on her face.

"What about Solomon?" I can tell she's trying to piece things together while remaining as calm as possible, struggling not to react but to look at things objectively. Her hand flexing on my leg would've clued me in, as well.

Jared shakes his head, his hair flopping over his eyes. "Solomon seldom leaves the library. I'm not joking, something is going on there, but we've had no luck figuring it out so far. We were busy trying to find you. They got to you before we did. With the wards around this apartment, I had to wait for Eric to leave so I could follow him in hopes he would let me see you. We couldn't get past the elevator in this place. We tried."

"Looking for me?" Jerking back, she looks from Jared, to me, then to Raphael. "You got them involved, and in danger?" Rounding on me, she takes me by surprise.

"He didn't know, Hel." Jared pulls her attention to him.

Good thing, too, because her hand relaxes on my thigh, and I can stop grinding my teeth. I fully expected my bone to snap. After Jared is done talking, I'll make sure Raphael sings like a canary. This is definitely not merely divine power. Raphael himself can't make me want to yelp in pain like she just did.

"Never mind." Huffing in frustration, she prompts him to keep talking, motioning with her hand. "What else did they say about Hector?"

"George was much closer to them. He told Cass and me that apparently, they are planning to send you a gift to make you willing to listen to them. He didn't know what they planned, just that it'll have something to do with Hector. But, none of us have seen Hector in a while, so I'm not sure how they can use him against you when he is not even around."

Helena looks at me, so many emotions playing one after another in her eyes until they settle on rage. Her green eyes burn with anger to seek justice for her father. I have every intention of helping her with that. The starting tremors of the building as a result of her rage are barely felt when she catches herself and concentrates on controlling her breathing.

"What else did they say?" Her voice is even, but she pushes the words through clenched teeth, not moving her eyes away from me.

"Um...nothing else important. Apart from some nonsense about angels being weak and not what they used to be. I'm not even sure that's what they said. George was pretty angry, so he might have heard wrong."

"Yeah." Helena drags the word out drily. "He must've heard wrong."

Turning away from me, Helena turns to Maddison first. Some unspoken conversations that none of the male kind will ever understand passes between the two women. Then she looks at Raphael. The Archangel nods, a slight tilt of his chin, acknowledging that he is ready for whatever she needs from him.

"Are you okay, Hel." Jared reaches his hand towards her

hesitantly, but thinks better of it, letting it drop between them on the sofa.

"Oh, I'm just peachy. And I think it's playtime." Her eyes glitter with excitement making my lips lift at the corners.

"Playtime it is then, cupcake." Winking, I get to my feet.

"You had to ruin it by calling me a cupcake, didn't you monster boy?"

Chuckling, I pull her to stand next to me. "You wouldn't want me to go easy on you, now would you? Besides, someone must keep you in line."

Chapter Twenty

HELENA

I appreciate Eric's efforts to keep things light, especially since I don't want Jared to see what kind of a freak I'm turning out to be. I'm no longer part of the team, so he has no reason to trust me. If I collapse this building on his head, I'm not sure Jared will be willing to do anything with me, much less help with finding Hector. As soon as he mentioned the patrons, my blood curdled in my veins. There was never love lost between the rest of them and my father. A blind person could've seen that their respect was based on fear of consequences. They wanted his position in the Order but were unwilling to let it show. For some reason, I never thought of any of them doing something foolish. Like actually hurting Hector. Now that I think of it, after an Archangel dismissed my father, they might be doing this to get in Michael's good graces. They might also be doing it as some twisted power play. If Adam is involved in it, the last thought might be spot on. I always thought there was something sadistic lurking behind his eyes.

Eric moves his hand up and down my back when I

shiver at my thoughts. Glancing around, I see everyone else still seated, watching me warily like I'm a ticking bomb. Filling my lungs with as much air as I can, I blow a raspberry in the air, making Eric chuckle.

"This is so messed up," saying it to no one in particular, I turn to Jared. "You should go back before you get in trouble. Tell George and Cass to be ready tonight. Meet us on the west side of Sanctuary in the wooded area. George will know the place, but just in case, tell him the same place Hector told us we would meet him the night before Michael snatched me away."

"Hel, you're not going anywhere near that place," Eric says calmly with so much authority in his voice one might think I'm his underling.

My head turns slowly in his direction, not missing Maddison grinning like a loon at his words. "And who will stop me, Eric? You?" With my full attention on him, I make sure he sees that I'm ready to win this argument. "Why don't you try and see how that goes for you."

"He might have a point." Raphael pipes in, sounding so hopeful I almost think he is sticking up for his best friend. "As I said a couple of times, I can go there to check."

"Any one of us can go check, which means you don't need to be there." Eric hasn't looked away from me, but I can tell that he understands the futility of this conversation.

He still tries, so I must give him credit for that.

"Because you know how to sneak inside? You know the layout of the place?" Shaking my head in disappointment at Eric, I turn to the Archangel in the room, "And how about you? When was the last time you were there, Holy one?"

"I thought Michael was the Holy whatever, not me," Raphael mumbles before pursing his lips. "It's been a while…"

"How long Raphael?" Making sure he understands I'm not in the mood for games, I raise my eyebrow in challenge.

"Since the day I accompanied Michael to drop you off to Hector as a baby." When I open my mouth to speak, he hurries to add his logic. "It can't be changed that much. I would've known if it was renovated because I would've been needed to set the wards, along with the others."

"You were planning to walk in through the front door?" Staring at him incredulously, I can't help but wonder if he really is insane. "You plan on walking in and doing what exactly? Calling a meeting and asking them where they are keeping Hector since you have his cut off hand to give back?"

"His what?" Jared's shout of surprise makes me groan. I need to stop letting my mouth run before my brain.

"His hand…" With a deep sigh, I press a hand to my forehead. "We were not sure it was his, but after what you told us, I'm willing to bet my father is definitely missing an appendage."

"Oh, dear God," Jared whispers, the color draining from his face as he covers his mouth with his hand.

"You haven't recovered yet, Hel. Let me do this while you at least take a day of not dealing with any of them. It might do you some good." Pulling me in his arms, Eric looks down at me. "I will not stop you from fighting them, just don't be stubborn when it comes to accepting help. Even I needed it, or I wouldn't have found you so soon," I can tell he admits that last part begrudgingly in front of Raphael. "Why are you being quiet right now when you always have a lot to say?" Turning, he glares at Maddison, taking his anger out on her because I'm refusing to obey him.

"Oh, I'm just here for the show." Grinning, she leans back on the sofa. "And the food."

"I'm going, Eric and there is nothing else to discuss. I'm a hunter. I've been doing this type of thing my whole life. And before you continue with all the reasons why I should stay behind, let me remind you that it's me they are all after. My life hangs in the balance, and that of my father. For all his shortcomings, Hector is a good man. I will go after him to try and save him before I receive any other body parts."

Jared whimpers.

Eric doesn't look happy, but he presses his lips in a thin line and nods sharply. Giddiness fills me at the prospect of finding Hector and making those that hurt him pay. My mind gets ahead of me, imagining all the ways I'm going to hurt Adam if he really is behind all this. He was there, too, when Amanda died, and he acted like he couldn't care less what happened to her. He even told me I was hallucinating, and the hunts were getting to me when I said that she was killed.

Thoughts like this would've sickened me not long ago. Hurting a human being was never on my bucket list, but surprisingly, I don't feel anything. Well, anything apart from the excitement and maybe some anxiety as well. Glancing around, I notice that there is no clock anywhere in the living room. Just the paintings on the walls with their burst of color in an otherwise black and white room.

"You don't have a clock here." I found it necessary to inform Eric of his lack of ordinary things to have. He looks at me like I've lost my mind.

"There is one hour left until sundown," Maddison informs me, sounding as official as a weather girl trying to impress a producer.

"Jared you should go." Making sure he understands the

gravity of the situation, I pull him to his feet. "You need to tell the others so you guys are ready if things go to shit and we need a hand. Tell George to meet us in the woods. One way or another, I'm getting inside the Sanctuary tonight, and God help the patrons if they are the ones that have hurt Hector. Demons will not be what they fear most after tonight."

Chapter Twenty-One

ERIC

After Jared reluctantly left, closing the door behind him like he just got a death sentence, Helena slumps on the sofa, curling into herself. Raphael opens his mouth, no doubt to begin spurting some nonsense in hopes to make her feel better—at least judging by the compassionate look on his face—but Maddison shakes her head at him, grabs his arm, and pulls him away from the living room. I keep watching my mate until their silhouettes disappear somewhere in the apartment. With a sigh, I gingerly sit next to her, not knowing what to say to make this better.

She looks small and lost, hugging her knees as she stares at nothing. It makes me want to rage and kill just so I never have to see her like this again. Pushing my anger aside, I pull her to me and wrap her in my arms.

"Hel…" The look she gives me stabs me in the heart like claws embedding into the muscle, ripping it to shreds and shriveling it to a husk. Full of despair and guilt, it does not belong on her beautiful face. But, what do I say to take it away?

"How did this happen, Eric?" She must've seen the slight crease of my eyebrows in my attempt to understand what exactly she's asking because she sighs, shakes her head, and looks out the window at nothing. "A couple of weeks ago, I was just a girl, you know? I had this purpose, this mission to keep the world safe. Part of the good guys, a family, a cog in something so much bigger than me, but needed to make everything work." Those green eyes focus back on my face, and I see the need there for me to tell her that it still stands true. I will not lie to her; things have never been as black and white as she was led to believe. "It was all a lie." Saying nothing, I don't shy away from her pain. "My life was a lie." She laughs humorlessly, rubbing a hand over her face with slow, tired movements.

"I think you give yourself too much credit on this one, Hel." She looks at me sharply like I've slapped her, but shaking my head, I smooth her hair away from her face. "You take responsibility for other people's actions. The only thing you've done is trust those that raised you. The ones that were supposed to protect you and love you just for you. Their motives and agendas are not your cross to bear, beautiful. You did nothing but stay true to your heart. You protected those that couldn't do it for themselves." Seeing her look at me doubtfully finally makes my lips tilt up in a small smile. "You were ridding the world of the rogues, weren't you?" She grimaces, but I can tell I have her attention, so I press more. "For all their shortcomings, they did one thing right. They taught you to survive, regardless if it was intentional or not. As much as I would like nothing more than to storm that damn place and put them all out of their misery, they kept you alive. I don't think you would've survived this long on your own, as much as it pains me to say it."

"Fewer people would've been hurt if I never found my way to the Sanctuary. I can tell myself things to feel better, but that's the ugly truth." Leaning her head on my shoulder, her trembling fingers are tracing circles on my chest. "Amanda would still be alive. Hector wouldn't be hurt and shunned from the people he dedicated his life to." She whispers the words with a raw, wobbly voice, making me swallow thickly.

"Did you kill your friend?"

"What?" She straightens to look at me, frowning. "I didn't do it, no, but it was because of me that she is dead, Eric. Nothing can change that."

"She died because of others' actions and agendas. You forget that I watched you on a few of your missions, Hel. How long do you think that girl would've stayed alive if you didn't stand between her and the rogues?" Her lips part, ready to argue her point, but I'll have none of that. It's time she knows what she has done for those that hunt her now. "I wasn't watching only you. Your team was good, yes. She was a good hunter. They were all very well trained very. They were not invincible! Yet, they stayed alive, all of them, thanks to you. What you are makes you better than an average hunter, no matter how blessed they are. You kept all of them alive. I'm not telling you to forget about her death. All I'm saying is you can't put it on your shoulders. You didn't kill her. They did. You want someone to blame for it? You have an entire group of assholes you can point your finger at, but never yourself."

I got her attention. She searches my face for a long time, unblinking. Watching her calmly, my hand moving up and down her back in a slow caress, I let her see that I genuinely mean it. They might not want her alive, but I'll be damned if I let them put all their sins on her. They will answer for their actions, one way or another. To me, or to my father, when they cross the veil and meet him face to face. I'll make sure of it.

"I wish it was that easy, to not feel responsible for everything that happened," she tells me after a while. "I understand what you are saying, but my heart doesn't accept it as an excuse. Not yet, anyway. It feels like if I accept what you are saying, her death means nothing. Hector's suffering means nothing. Someone needs to take responsibility for it, to acknowledge that their lives matter, and I'm willing to do that for them."

"But not with guilt, Hel. Never with guilt." Taking her face in my hands, I kiss her until her eyes go unfocused. "You want what happened to matter? I need Helena back. The kick-ass, smart-mouthed hunter that took my breath away the first time my eyes landed on her. *She* will hold everyone accountable for their actions. *She* will collect the dues owed to those she loves. Don't let them take her from me, Hel. Not just you, I need her as well."

Tears spill down her cheeks at my words. A trembling hand lifts to my face and she smiles sadly. I'm prepared to keep talking, to say whatever comes from deep inside my heart, to tell this woman that turned my life inside out something that might stop her tears, but all the words get stuck in my throat when the dull look in her green eyes disappears. Like emeralds, they start sparkling with determination and anger, taking my breath away.

"Thank you!" Kissing me stupid, making me blink a few times after she pulls away so I can get my brain back into gear, Helena grins wickedly at me. "You are right! I will not let them destroy me inside. If they try to break me, I'll just fight harder. And thanks to you, I know what I want to do now."

"Go kick some righteous ass?" Smirking, I tangle my hands in her hair, tilting her face up. "Playtime for the she-devil?"

"Revenge, Eric." The power she packs in her words shakes me to my core like I've been kicked by a bull, goose-flesh covers me from head to toe. "They will pay for what they did. I want revenge!"

She lifts herself off the sofa, squaring her shoulders and smiling down at my stupefied face. I wanted to take away the pain she felt for everything that's been happening to her after that night when her friend died. Looking at her right now, I'm not sure, but I think I might have opened Pandora's box. The woman standing in front of me is ready to bring Heaven and Hell down to their knees. Power pulses out of her like strong waves of an ocean, causing me to take slow, shallow breaths from the intensity. I accept the hand she has reached out to help me to my feet, but my mind is spinning. I hope I didn't create a monster.

Hell is paved with good intentions, my mind supplied John Ray's quote as if mocking me... There is only one way to find out how true that is.

Chapter Twenty-Two

HELENA

Eric's words play on repeat in my head, fueling my determination. I'm not sure when, somewhere along the way, Michael managed to screw my head up but he obviously did. It's not a big revelation what Eric said. It's evident to anyone with a brain, yet I kept drowning in my pain and guilt with not even a straw to grasp onto and keep my head above it.

Warmth spreads in my chest like the first warm breeze of spring after a long, harsh winter. Eric is watching me warily, like I've grown horns or something. My lips stretch wide all the way to my ears, seeing the Prince of Hell being worried because of little ol' me. It might come off as a drastic change from one blink of an eye to the next to him, but I find it easy to flip that switch inside me and see this whole clusterfuck for what it is.

Mind games.

The Order and the Archangel are powerful beyond measure. There is no question about it. What they did, however, is they made sure I forgot that they are trying to eliminate me because I am powerful in my own right. They wouldn't have bothered with everything they've done if that wasn't true. By being on the defensive the entire time, they made sure I didn't see through their tactics. Tactics that worked well for them, until now that is. Hurt or kill those around me, hunt me to keep me looking over my shoulder with every breath I take. Worry about the rest of those I care about. Eric's words cleared the fog around my mind so that I can see clearly in this cat and mouse chase, instead of wandering aimlessly, blind to everything.

I was predictable. That was my downfall.

Time to show them how this abomination can play!

"Maybe we should talk about this, Hel." Pulling Eric up to his feet, my lips twitch at his wariness, "When we let emotions guide our actions, we make mistakes. Sometimes important ones that we can't take back." Searching my face, he looks troubled, making my heart melt when I see how much he cares. "I should know all about those mistakes..." he mumbles under his breath.

"I'm not going on a killing spree, monster boy!" Laughing at his frown, I kiss his full lips, unable to pass up the opportunity. "I'm just going to play a little. This mouse is about to turn the tables on the cat. Won't that be fun?"

"I'm all for you having fun, Hel cat. I'm right there with you. I am a demon, after all." Smiling wickedly at me, he pulls me harshly to his chest. Wariness creeps up in his gaze again when he looks down at me, his hurt thumping fast under my fingertips that are pressed against his chest. "I just don't want you to act rashly and do things you will regret later. Especially since we don't yet understand this new power coming out of you in waves."

"I don't have time to explore new powers, no matter

what they are. Hector needs me now, not next week."
Glaring at him, I push gently on his chest.

Eric flies back, his ass hitting the sofa behind him, skidding a few feet back with it. Gasping, I stare dumbly from him to my raised hands, wide-eyed. I would've thought this was his way of trying to get me to slow down with my plans, acting as if I hurt him, but the incredulous look on his face tells me otherwise. He definitely did not expect it, just like me. Eric is still sitting on the askew sofa, his hands firmly pressed on the leather, his legs spread wide and planted on the floor, checking me strangely. Taking a deep breath to say —I have no idea what to say to him at this point—my mouth opens and closes a few times before a peel of feminine laughter makes both of us jerk our heads sharply to look at Maddison.

"Oh, my!" Leaning against the entrance to the kitchen with one shoulder, her arms folded over her chest, she has a Cheshire cat smile stretching her red lips. "You two should see the looks on your faces right now!" Throwing her head back, she keeps laughing like this is all a joke to her.

Not like my life hit a new speed like a rollercoaster ride from my worst nightmares.

"What happened?" Raphael pokes his head out above Maddison. They look funny standing next to each other, him with his six-foot-five frame and Maddison barely above five-foot-five, and all curvy like any man's wild, wet dreams.

"Helena just showed Eric who wears the pants in the relationship." Gasping for air, she sweeps her fingers under her eyes and wipes the tears away. "I would've paid to see this!"

"This is so not funny!" Managing to squeeze the words through my numb lips, I gingerly walk towards Eric. "I'm…" Clearing my throat and ignoring Maddison's continuing laughter, I swallow the lump that lodged there. "I'm sorry, Eric. I have no idea what I did."

"You did nothing, Hel." Finally lifting himself off the sofa, he looks at it, grimacing. "It's that asshole's fault." Stabbing an accusing finger at Raphael, he takes a threatening step towards him. "He fucking mixed his fingers where they don't belong!"

"I did no such thing…" Raphael stutters, but Maddison laughs harder, silencing all of us to stare at her like she's lost her mind. "You think she's okay?" Stepping away from her like she is a ticking bomb, the Archangel inches his way towards Eric and I.

"You and Eric are stupid!" Her laughter stops, and Maddison glares at Raphael like he insulted her. "It's either that, or I have no idea what to say to the two of you."

"What are you talking about?" Eric growls at her, clenching his fists harder the closer Raphael comes to where we are standing.

Ignoring him, as is her habit I've noticed, she looks me up and down. I squirm. "How old are you, Helena?"

The question is so out of left field that my brain short-circuits for a split second. I answer automatically, out of habit when someone asks a simple question. A passerby says, "How are you?" your automatic response is "Fine, and you?" even if you are not fine at all. "I'm twenty-one."

Maddison smirks, watching pointedly first Raphael, then Eric. They stare at her, confused along with me, because apparently, I'm stupid too since I don't get it either. Slapping a hand on her forehead with a resounding slap, she huffs a breath and shakes her head. "Let's sit. This is one of those things I guess I have to explain, although it should be obvious to these two knuckleheads." Waving a manicured hand with red painted nails at the men, she strides and sits primly on the sofa that I didn't push away with my new She-Hulk ability.

Eric pulls the sofa back towards the coffee table, Raphael and him sitting on it next to each other, forcing me to suppress a laugh. They look like children at the principal's office after they got into trouble. Their dislike of each other forgotten, bonding in hopes to get out of whatever trouble they're in. Since we are acting like five-year old's, I go and sit next to Maddison, making her grin at me, which she follows with a wink.

"Well, children." Clapping her hands like a teacher, Maddison smiles demurely at them. I burst out laughing but stifle it down after a second. Waving a hand for her to continue, I close my mouth biting the inside of my lips. "We have obviously forgotten that our dear Helena here"—one of her hands moves up and down in my direction like I'm a specimen in an exhibit— "is not a human, regardless of how she's been raised." She looks at Eric and Raphael expectantly. "No? Nothing?" Groaning, Maddison twists her lips in displeasure. "She's twenty-one, you idiots. Raphael was right that she was feeding off him while Michael had her in that awful place. He was wrong that he was making her more 'angelic,' however. She was only replenishing her own energy because she was depleted with what was happening to her. I'm sure Michael didn't help with it either. She's been coming into her powers since her birthday. I'm sure this is not the first thing that popped up." Turning to me, she watches me intently. "Anything unusual happen since your birthday before this?" At my confused face, she clarifies, "Any dizziness, bursts of energy? Unexplainable things happening?"

Eric and Raphael perk up at her words, turning to each other with a look on their faces that says, "Oh, yeah," but

I'm still confused. "Uhm…I can't think of anything off the top of my head." And just like always in situations like this, my mind supplies unhelpful reminders of everything unusual that has happened.

Maddison was frowning, but at my guilty look, she perks up. "What was it?" Leaning eagerly towards me, she grabs both my hands in hers.

Doing my best not to glance at Eric, I keep my focus on her. "Apart from actually fainting a couple of times, which I thought was from anxiety…actually, now that you mention it, I'm not so sure it was that. There were a couple of other things too." Squirming, my heart is beating like a hammer against my ribs. "The rogues stopped trying to kill me. They were trying to capture me. I thought it was because of the blood that one of them got from me, but now that I think on it, it started right before that. And I was also able to see other demons, not just the rogues. Until the night Amanda died, I've never seen anything but the rogues."

With a satisfied smirk, Maddison releases my hands and folds hers in her lap, then she shoots the two men an arrogant glance. Raphael looks like he has swallowed a hot potato, his yellow eyes pulsing with light. Eric, on the other hand, watches me intently through a narrowed gaze, like he is trying to see through a glamour I've put on myself. Glaring at him, I lift my chin defiantly. The wicked grin that spreads on his face makes me almost slide into a puddle on the floor.

Chapter Twenty-Three

ERIC

Maddison has an excellent point. I am stupid for not realizing this straight away. I was going to tell her again that there is a reason why she is the brains of our operations, but the arrogance coming off her at the moment changes my mind. I'll be hearing about this for years to come, so I might as well keep it to a minimum. I think Helena was expecting to get a reaction like the one she received from the Order when her bloodline was revealed. She couldn't be more wrong.

This changes everything.

Blowing a breath through pursed lips, she looks at Maddison for answers. It eats at my pride that my mate can't turn to me, but I don't blame her. My own stupidity and acting before thinking brought us here. She is wise to look at my cousin for help. I also feel the Archangel next to me practically quivering in his attempt to stay quiet.

"So, what does all this mean?" Glancing at us, Helena wiggles in her seat to better face Maddison.

"It will take a full year or two until your strongest attributes show themselves." Tilting her head left and right, Madison sighs. "That is the case for demons and angels alike. I'm hoping it's the same for you, but…you are a *special* case, for lack of a better word. You have both traits, which means you're either the same as the rest of us, or we will get surprises as we go."

"Great!" A frown forms on Helena's forehead "I'm the freak amongst the freaks. I can't even get that right."

"You are not a freak!" Raphael bursts out next to me, and I almost jump out of my skin. Turning to glare at him does nothing because he wouldn't take his eyes off my mate.

"Says you, one of the Holy asses." Waving a hand dismissively at him, Helena stays lost in her thoughts.

Maddison snorts.

"Michael is the Holy ass. I'm just Holy," Raphael says, defensively making Maddison laugh outright, and even Helena's lips twitch at that.

"Touché, Holy one, touché." Smiling at him, my mate locks her gaze on mine. "No comment, monster boy? You got stuck with the queen of freaks. How unfortunate for you."

"But you forget one thing, she-devil. You're my freak." I know my eyes are pulsing with amber light because she does that to me.

"You must know how messed up that sounds when the son of Lucifer tells you that you are 'his freak.'" Her lips curl slightly at that but it's gone in an instant. "All joking aside, what now?" Glancing from one of us to the next, Helena wipes her hands on her thighs. "I don't have time to wait for whatever it is going to manifest. Hector doesn't have the time."

"You'll be okay, Helena." Maddison cuts me off when I open my mouth. "We will take it one step at a time and guide you." Glancing sideways at Raphael, amusement dances in her gaze. "We are more than equipped for it in this unlikely band of brothers in arms."

"We will deal with it as it comes, Hel. Now that we know what's going on." Beaming, I give her a reassuring nod. "You'll be fine. I have no doubt."

"You seem to always have more faith in me than I do." Her words are soft like she's not aware that she spoke out loud. "All this is taking too long; the daylight is almost gone. What's our plan? First, get Hector out, then meet Michael?"

"I think it's best to go that route. I know you won't be at your best if you keep thinking about what Hector is going through." Remembering my earlier question, I lean my forearms on my knees, making sure I don't miss a twitch of her muscles. "Why aren't your guns on you? You didn't want them further than an arm's reach."

Shifting uneasily on the sofa, Helena stares at the coffee table for long moments before turning to me. "I don't know, Eric." Her distressed look makes my gut tighten "When I touched them after you guys got me out of that cursed, loony place, I felt nothing. I always felt calm when my skin touched the metal, or when the weight of them was in my hands. But, now…" Shaking her head, puzzled, she glances at Raphael as if she's uncomfortable saying it in front of him. "They are made with blessed metal, using blessed bullets and all. Yet, I felt nothing. Like they are not my guns, although I know they are. I thought maybe the demon in me is stronger than the angel, at least that's how I explained it to myself. Whatever it is, they'll be useless to me now. The bond is broken…it's the only way I can explain it."

"That's ridiculous!" Raphael growls, leaning towards her as well. "The powers manifesting now are angelic."

"Are they now?" Maddison pipes in, shooting daggers at the Archangel through her eyes. "And who said that? You?"

"Guys!" Helena snaps, cutting off the argument that was about to start. "I'm not a damn toy for you to argue over. Geez! It's my life we are talking about!" Glaring at both of them, she shocks me, even more, when her green eyes pulse with a strange light, something between amber and gold, like liquid fire. "Can we focus on not arguing and help the freak?" Taking a deep breath, she releases it slowly "Please!"

"You don't need the guns." I surprise myself as well as her. "You are well trained. Don't you remember how many hunters you put out of commission with a mop handle?" Her lips twitch at my words, but there is fear lurking in her gaze that doesn't sit well with me. "The guns are just an object that you used to center yourself. To concentrate on doing what you do best. You don't need them. What you need is to stop doubting yourself. And stop worrying if you are more demon or angel. You are Helena. That's all that needs to matter."

"Was he always this philosophical?" Not looking away from me, Helena asks Maddison. I glare at her.

"No, I can't say he was." Musing, Maddison gives me a scrutinizing look. "I think you bring that out in him. Who would've thought? Ha! The king of 'I don't give a damn' was wise somewhere deep inside."

"We don't have time for you to make fun of me!" Squeezing the words through clenched teeth, I turn my glare from Helena to Maddison. When together, these two will be the death of me. "That being said—" Without warning, my arm shoots out, fast as lightning, punching Raphael square in the face and flinging him off the sofa. "Ahhhh… that felt good!"

"You miserable exc—" Raphael's angry growl cuts off, probably remembering that he is an angel and cussing is not something the righteous assholes do.

"That's for pissing me off all day." Lifting myself off the same sofa the sprawled Archangel shared with me until a moment ago, I pull a stunned Helena to her feet. "You're expending too much energy because of all these new powers manifesting. You need food." I start dragging her towards the kitchen. She must still be stunned from me punching Raphael because she follows me without argument. "Let's get something in your belly."

"I'm all for food if you're cooking!" Maddison jumps up and follows us excitedly, snickering when she walks past Raphael.

"I will get you back for this demon. Don't you worry." Lifting himself off the floor, Raphael reluctantly joins us, rubbing his jaw.

"Yeah, yeah. I'm sure we haven't seen the last of you yet." Glancing over my shoulder, I smirk at him before pulling a chair and pushing Helena to sit. "You are known for your vicious fighting, after all." Chuckling at my mocking tone and his reddening face, I turn to the fridge and begin pulling foodstuffs to feed my mate.

We all eat, lost in our own thoughts. I keep glancing at Helena, but she doesn't notice. Her eyes keep flicking from side to side, her mind going through everything that was said no doubt. I let her process it all without disturbance, glaring bloody murder every time Maddison or Raphael open their mouths to break the silence. Wisely, they keep quiet, staring at their plates. When Helena finishes her food, I push my plate away and grab her hand, guiding her to the bedroom. She is watching me questionably but allows me to lead her away. After closing the door to the world, I hug her to my chest for a long moment before making sure she is laying down on top of the covers. One of her eyebrows goes up when I'm still standing next to the bed and haven't ripped her clothes off to shreds.

"You need to rest, too." I know what's coming and I'm prepared for it now.

Her eyes narrow angrily at me as a wave of power slams into me like a bull.

"Don't you dare or you'll pay for it!" She pushes on her elbows, trying to lift herself up, but I'm faster.

"Sleep." My voice is deeper than usual, and her lids flutter before closing. "I know you'll make sure I pay for it," I tell my sleeping mate, kissing her forehead while inhaling her scent. "I'll gladly pay whatever you need, as long as you are at the top of your game."

Chapter Twenty-Four

HELENA

Watching the city of Atlanta pass in a blur through the window of the SUV, my mind keeps going back to everything Maddison said. Whoever it is that is creating our destinies, or fates—whatever you want to call it—must be a bigger bitch than karma. Like I didn't have enough on my plate right now, I had to be going through some transition, or transformation, like some larva coming out of a cocoon. A grunt from the back seat makes me glance at Maddison.

She is driving, and I'm sitting shotgun, leaving Eric and Raphael in the back seat. After the jerk made me sleep against my will, he is in the doghouse. Hence, he had to begrudgingly climb up in the back next to Raphael. Although the vehicle is large enough to have a soccer match in the back, it's not big enough for both their egos to fit nicely inside. As toddlers, they keep pushing, shifting, and elbowing each other, and they've been doing it ever since we left the parking lot of Eric's building.

An ungraceful snort escapes my lips, followed by one coming from Maddison at the shifting, then another grunt

134

from the children in the back. Since I woke up, after a few hours of sleep that I needed but would never admit to needing, I made it my mission to make him suffer.

Successfully so far, I might add.

Changing my clothing to fit my new mood accordingly, I waltzed out of that bedroom. Dressed in leather pants that hugged my body like a second skin, a black tank top layered on top of a white one—symbolic for my half-demon half-angel bloodline—a leather vest tight around my waist, and calf-high black boots pointy enough to be used as a cold weapon if needed. All that just to irk him; it's been fun. I've been feeling his intent gaze like a physical caress all over my body, his glowing amber orbs following me like the predator tracking prey. It makes my blood pump faster through my veins, warmth spreading all over me. I might've put an exaggerated sway to my hips just to gloat as part of his punishment. He will think twice before doing something stupid like that again.

Eric managed to surprise me as well. He changed out of his trademark leather pants, wearing jeans that are sitting low on his hips and, as usual, a tank top hugging his torso, outlining every dip and curve of his muscles. I pinch my forearms a few times to snap out of it when I catch myself following his body movements. Luckily for me, he didn't see it. I'm still winning this game. For now.

"Again, why are we going to your office first?" Raphael sounds pained, my smile stretching from his discomfort.

"I made a few calls and I need to pick up something important before we storm the Order." Grinning at me, Maddison does her best not to show it in her voice. She sounds dead serious.

Eric mumbles something unintelligible, huffing and puffing like the wolf in front of the piglet's house. I have to force myself not to allow my shoulders to shake when all I want to do is laugh. A few minutes later, we turn into the parking garage where I first met Maddison. The tension in the car skyrockets when she guns the SUV, heading straight for the wall. With a quick glance over my shoulder, I see the horrified expression on Raphael's face, much like my own when Eric brought me here, I imagine. His eyes squeeze shut for a while before one eyelid peels open. Both his eyes open wide and he leans between the two front seats to stare around us. Eric is not happy about the Archangels reaction, but that doesn't seem to faze Raphael at the moment. He looks like a kid taken to Disneyland for the first time.

"Don't forget to breathe, Raphael." Laughing, I slap his face playfully. He grins at me eagerly.

"I always wondered how they stayed off the radar, and we can never pinpoint where they were." Still smiling, he keeps twisting his neck to look around at everything at once.

"It better stay that way if you want to keep your feathers!" Eric growls from behind me.

"I would never tell a soul, demon." Raphael sounds insulted, his smile slipping off his angelic face.

"You can't help but be a party popper, monster boy. Can you?" Unable to pass up the opportunity, I make a jab at him.

I don't hear everything he says, apart from this not being a joke, because Maddison parks and we jump out of the vehicle. Raphael scrambles out from the back, no doubt eager to see more. Eric, on the other hand, slams his door with a lot more force than necessary, walking purposely towards me. Instinctively, I try to move faster before I catch myself.

"You'll pay for this." Snatching my arm and pulling me to him, he growls deep in his throat, turning my legs to jelly.

Summoning all the strength inside me, enough to make women worldwide proud for resisting the delicious specimen next to me, I purse my lips. "I seem to remember that *you* are the one paying for it, monster boy." Lifting one eyebrow, staring pointedly at his hand wrapped around my arm, I start peeling it from my skin with two fingers. "No touchy-feely for you after making me do things against my will."

"Helena." There is a warning in the way he says my name, but I turn on my heels, strutting away from him.

"Come, boy!" Glancing over my shoulder, I slap my hand a couple of times on my thigh, the leather making a snapping sound echo around the quiet parking lot as if I'm calling a pet. His green eyes turn amber, and I almost stumble from the hunger staring at me from their depths.

Maddison laughs joyfully as she walks towards the glass double doors, and I hurry after her like she can save me from the demon setting his sights on me. When I reach the doors close enough to be able to see the lobby, a frown forms between my eyebrows. Loren glares at me a moment before all the blood drains from her face, and moving faster than I thought her able, she disappears in the hallway to our right. She can't still hate me for being Eric's mate, can she? Turning around to see if Eric had something to do with her reaction, I'm just in time to see Raphael colliding into his back. The Archangel's head was swiveling around, not paying attention before bumping into Eric.

"That woman is starting to get on my nerves." Maddison slows down and tells me conversationally, just as we walk through the glass doors that parted in front of us.

"Yeah." Still not understanding her reaction, I glance at Maddison. "I'm not sure she likes me much." Smiling to not show my discomfort, I wave a hand between us. "Not that I care, mind you. I have enough shit to deal with without her."

Nodding, Maddison stays quiet after that, and I forget all about it when we reach the second set of doors. We walk through the creepy hallway with no sound, like a sound-proof chamber. I can feel Raphael's anxiety around us, and notice Eric's nostrils flare as he glances at the Archangel. My feet move faster to reach the doors at the end. It's unsettling to not even hear our footsteps on the tiles. We practically spill inside Maddison's office as soon as we reach it in our rush.

"Ah! It's here!" She claps her hands excitedly, rushing to her desk.

My feet slow down until I freeze in place, staring at her open mouthed. Looking at Raphael and Eric, I'm grateful that I'm not the only one shocked to the point of stupidity. Maddison, without a care in the world, lifts the curved dagger from her desk gingerly, like she's holding some priceless artifact and lifting it for us to see. It feels like we just entered *The Avatar*, the curved blade resembling the Na' vi daggers. Smiling from ear to ear, she's almost vibrating with excitement.

"This is for you," she tells me, my mouth unhinging more, if that is possible. "It belonged to your father."

Chapter Twenty-Five

ERIC

Holding myself back so I don't rip Maddison to pieces, I clench my fists. She means well; I know that, but she didn't hear Helena telling me she wants revenge. Now, here we are with Maddison handing her a weapon that belonged to a demon of vengeance. It's too much of a fucked-up situation for this to be a coincidence. Do I prevent her from touching it, or should I let the web unravel as the fates see fit?

Raphael is standing next to me, coiled up like a spring ready to snap, leaning on the balls of his feet. For the umpteenth time, my mind wonders why he is here, however, at this moment, I'm hoping his presence will be the conscience the rest of us are lacking and it'll stop Helena taking that blade. I almost nudge him to speak, but he beats me to it.

"I'm not sure that's a smart thing to do." He sounds pained, and his voice is strained.

I glare at Maddison. She pointedly ignores me.

"It's her right to carry it. She needs a weapon anyway." My cousin sounds reasonable, like a witch luring you to bite an apple. That thought is like a bucket of cold water dumped on my head.

"Stop!" My yell is like a whip, stopping Helena's fingers an inch from touching the blade. She looks at me over her shoulder, her green eyes wide. "We don't know if that's your father's. Demonic weapons are not something to play with lightly." My murderous glare will freeze anyone in their tracks.

Maddison rolls her eyes. "It belonged to her father, Eric." Waving the blade now clutched in one of her hands, she points it at me. "Only one vengeance demon has died in the last thirty years. Want to guess which one of them is her father?" Her eyebrows climb up her forehead, mocking me. "Plus, I'm touching it dumbass. It's just a blade! A sharp thingy that can save her life if she needs it, I might add." She makes few jabbing motions in the air, demonstrating the stabbing part of her comment.

I move at the same time as Helena, but she is too close to Maddison. My fingers curl around her arm at the same time as hers wrap around the handle of the blade. Helena hisses in pain but doesn't let go of the dagger. The red leather handle shimmers for a second before the curved blade begins glowing. At first faintly, but the longer she holds it, the brighter the deep red glow is. Symbols are appearing on the blade, easily noticeable by their golden light. Raphael's sharp intake of breath makes my head snap in his direction.

The Archangel looks pale, and with all the blood drained from his face, he resembles a statue. His mouth is opening and closing, but no sound is coming out. His yellow eyes turn to liquid gold, losing their similarity to human eyes. One of his arms is stretched in front of him, as if he wanted to stop Helena before she touched the blade. But he was too late, and it was all for nothing.

Turning back to Helena, I search her face. She ignores all of us, intently studying the weapon in her hand. Her wrist moves this way and that, examining it before testing its weight in her hand. Slowly, she lifts her head up and looks at me. The office is as quiet as the hallway leading here.

I'm holding my breath.

"I like it." Smiling happily at me, Helena moves her wrist in circular motions, testing the blade more. "It freaked me out at first." With a whoosh, I release my breath a moment too soon. "I think it bit me."

"WHAT?" My roar makes everyone flinch, including me.

Helena dances away from me, wrenching her arm free from my grip when I try to snatch the blade from her hand. Raphael seems ready to pass out, so I ignore him. Maddison looks from me to Helena with a shocked look on her face. Rounding on her, my hand grabs her delicate throat, lifting her off her feet.

"I told you not to give her the cursed blade." She doesn't fight me, goosebumps popping out on her arms at the sound of my voice.

I squeeze harder, angry enough to kill her for hurting Helena. Then, a mind-numbing pain blooms on my side, sending me crashing into the opposite wall. I must've released Maddison because I'm crumpled and disoriented all by myself next to the obviously sturdy wall. Not even dust falls on me from it. Shaking my head to clear it, I look up just in time to see my mate helping my cousin to her feet. Helena even glares at me before fretting over Maddison like she's a human that was just attacked by a demon. The demon being me, obviously.

"What the hell is the matter with you, Eric?!" Spitting the words angrily, Helena looks Maddison up and down one more time before fully turning to me. "You are out of control. We are killing each other now?"

And it's that moment that my brain got back online. Lifting myself off the floor, I watch Helena glare at me with her arms crossed over her stomach, pushing her breasts up. "Did you just hit me, cupcake?"

"I've also shot you twice, but you never complained before. And I wasn't the one on the floor so I'd reconsider using the word cupcake." Smirking, her gaze sweeps me, as if checking for injuries. Throwing my head back, I laugh. "I will do it again if you attack either one of them." Her glare is back, but I keep chuckling. "There is nothing funny here!"

"Sorry." Snickering a couple more times, coughing to cover it up with no success, I shake my head. "I might've overreacted a little." When her glare turns deadly, I amend, "A lot." She huffs but doesn't move away from her place between Maddison and me. "You can't blame me. After our talk earlier, I didn't know what to expect. And you said it bit you. Let me see."

"They must've known the blade would find its way to her." Raphael's words stop me from reaching for the blade. We all turn to the Archangel that is still ashen, resembling a statue with glowing, golden eyes.

"What are you talking about?" Maddison comes around her desk to stand next to Helena and I. "It's a blade, no matter the light show."

"Those are angelic sigils on a demonic blade, Maddison. No one but her could've activated them." His head tilts, the only indication that he is watching Helena since he has no irises or pupils. "You said it bit you, yes? It must've drawn blood. Your power had to have activated it."

"How is that possible." I've never heard of anything like this in all my centuries. "More importantly, how do you know about it?"

"Her mother mentioned it to me before she died. Like she knew her days were numbered. I thought it was some nonsense the demon was feeding her to keep her at his side."

"Exactly how close were you to my mother, angel?" Helena takes the words out of my mouth.

Raphael shakes his head as if clearing it before his eyes turn back to normal, pulling himself out of the shock. "That is a very long story." Watching Helena warily, he clears his throat. "I will tell you everything you want to know, but I thought we needed to get to your earthly father fast. We wouldn't want to leave him to suffer so I can tell you tales from times past."

Helena straightens her shoulders just as the Archangel knew she would. He ignores my glare. Maddison and I exchange a glance, but my mate is already moving. I'll find out what the feathered asshole is hiding if it's the last thing I do.

"Let's go!" Pulling the door open, almost ripping it off the hinges, Helena bolts out of the room like it's on fire. "There will be time to talk later. We must get Hector."

I follow right on her heels, passing the Archangel. "Whatever it is you are hiding, pray to your creator it doesn't hurt my mate. Neither Heaven, nor Hell, will be big enough to hide you from me."

I see him flinch and nod solemnly at me before I disappear through the door.

Chapter Twenty-Six

HELENA

The air in the SUV is thicker than before. It's almost painful to breathe with the testosterone oozing out of Eric in spades. Part of me melts at his protective side, pushing me to go hide and squeal in delight.

Like an idiot.

The other part, thankfully much stronger and smarter, wants me to punch him in the face for acting like a caveman. Or like I have no brain, needing him to tell me what's right for me. I can't blame him because of everything that happened, but I'm not happy about it. It makes me feel like a burden. Someone he needs to continually look after, like a toddler.

I watch the metal bars of the familiar decoration stretching up towards the dark sky holding the symbolic peach for Georgia between them as we exit Atlanta, heading towards the Sanctuary. The traffic thins around us, only an occasional vehicle passing on either side of I-75. Trees stretch in a never-ending line to our right, giving me a peaceful feeling despite the tension around me. I understand

Eric's reaction. I don't like it, and I'll have to talk to him about it, but now is not the time. So, pushing those thoughts aside, I look down at the dagger I'm still holding in my hand like someone might take it from me.

"You okay?" Maddison asks softly, for my ears only.

Not looking away from the blade, I barely nod my head a few times. I think I'm okay, which is a lot more than Hector can say. When I first touched the handle of the dagger, it freaked me out when I felt it pinch my palm. Switching hands, I look at the tiny hole at the center. It drew blood before it started glowing, flooding me with so much power I felt my skin might burst from it. Feeling dizzy for a moment, grinding my teeth, I kept breathing slowly, not to freak out the other three people in the room. What seemed like an eternity later, but it was only a second or two surely, it balanced itself out and felt like it was part of me. Not like my guns were; this is much deeper, more personal. The weight of it was like regaining the movement of your arm after it being numb for hours. Painful, yet pleasant. A gift left from my parents before they parted with their lives. Could they have known that I would survive the wrath of the Archangels?

Turning my head slowly to the side, hoping no one will notice what I'm doing, I glance at Raphael in the back seat. I can't make out his features, just a dark silhouette in the shadows, but I can tell he is sitting still as a statue. Not moving a muscle. The answers lay with him, I know that much. Fortunately for him, because he looks reluctant to share his story, we've wasted enough time with my melt-down and Eric's caveman behavior. I'll have to get to the bottom of it after we get Hector to safety.

Lost in my thoughts, I didn't realize how much time has passed. When I look out the window, the familiar secluded road meets my gaze, twisting and turning between tall, thick trees. The headlights turn off, plunging us into darkness. My heart jackhammers in my chest while my hand clutches the blade in a tight grip, and I blink few times trying to adjust, seeing only with the moon as a guide. The silvery glow peeks in and out between the tops of the trees we are passing. I almost scream when Eric's fingers grip my shoulder. A pathetic yelp escapes, unfortunately.

"We will get him out, Hel." I can hear the laughter he is hiding clear in his voice at the embarrassing sound I made. "Let's just not act rashly, that way we don't hurt the innocent bystanders."

My anger spikes, remembering all the hunters responsible for the destruction of the home Eric and Maddison built for their kind when Michael took me. They don't feel like bystanders to me. I tell them as much. My words are like an ax hitting the executioner's block just before the head thumps to the ground. It's almost as if no one is breathing.

"Don't blame them for something they may not have control over, Helena," Raphael speaks for the first time. "My brother can be very persuasive when he wants something as badly as he wants you."

"You forget I was there, Archangel." Turning to see him over my shoulder, I make sure he knows I'm not going to allow them to get away with hurting those that haven't done anything wrong. There were children there for God's sake, regardless if they were demon or human. "I fought them, and they looked very lucid to me."

"I'm not saying for you to let them hurt you. I'm just saying they might be misguided in some matters." He says tiredly.

The SUV comes to a stop, my patience flying out the

door. Pushing the door open, I stop, my body half outside, half inside the vehicle. "I'm the last person you should worry about hurting innocents, Raphael. But know one thing." Turning to look him dead in the eyes, I see him stiffen. "Anyone that has hurt Hector is fair game to me. He raised most of them, feeding them and wiping their tears while growing up alongside me. If they don't know what's right, or wrong, I'll make sure to teach them tonight."

Jumping out of the car, gently pushing the door closed so I don't announce our presence if patrols are nearby, I turn in a circle, looking around. Eric comes to my back, his arms circling my waist and pulling me into the warmth of his body. Allowing myself a moment of weakness, I lean on him, relishing his nearness. Who knows what we will come across tonight. I'll enjoy this moment as much as I can. His head comes down, his breath tickling the skin on my neck before his warm lips press on the carotid artery pulsing wildly there. "I got you, Hel." His lips skim the surface of my skin when he speaks. "You are not doing this alone. Where you go, I go. We will get him out."

"I know." Speaking just as softly, I squeeze his forearms encircling me in gratitude. "I just don't know what we will find when we get to him."

"We are talking about Hector." Turning me around so I'm facing him, Eric looks sternly at me. "The old man that had balls of steel when he came to me and asked me to kill his daughter. Even knowing that I wouldn't be able to do it. No matter what they've done, as long as he is breathing, the old goat will be fine. You'll see."

I can't help but smile at that. Eric has a point. I think my stubbornness comes from Hector, even if he is not blood. Knowing that he will pull through no matter what makes me stand straighter. Eric grins proudly at me, so I punch him in the gut just because.

"So violent for a half angel." He chuckles, but he is grinding his teeth, making me grin at him.

"Helena!" Jared hissing my name from behind one of the trees puts my mind back on track.

"Jared?" Quickly glancing around, I run towards him, the rest of our group following fast. "Why are you here? I told you to ask George to meet us!"

Jared looks over his shoulder as if expecting Michael to pop out from behind a tree. Anxiety ricochets to new heights inside me. "They dragged George out kicking and screaming while I was telling him what you said." Gulping, his wide, panicked eyes look glazed with terror. "They said he was possessed, and he needs to be locked up or put down for our safety. I couldn't help him. I stood there watching them drag him away, Hel."

He is horrified, shaking like a leaf. "Where is Cass, Jared?" Grabbing his shoulders, I shake him to make him snap out of it. "Look at me, Jared! Where is Cass?"

"I don't know…" his words trail off as if it is the first time remembering his girlfriend. I frown at him.

"What are you playing at Jared?" Releasing him, I take a step away from him.

His face transforms from terrified to gloating in a blink of an eye. Black spots are dancing at the corners of my eyes. "Not so tough now, Helena, are you?"

His words are followed by a sea of hunters coming from everywhere. The four of us press back to back, making sure we don't have a blind spot. The pathetic asshole sold us out. Glaring at him, I hope he understands that I will enjoy every moment it takes to break every single bone in his body.

"Why?" Unable to let it go, I must know why he did this. "Don't you remember what they did to Amanda? What they are doing to Hector?"

"Why?" Hissing, Jared takes a step towards me, but Eric's feral growl makes him run back a few steps. "I'll be an elite now, you stupid cow. Michael will bestow power and gifts upon me when I bring you to him. I will never be helpless again, waiting on the rest of you to keep me alive."

"You poor fool." Maddison chuckles humorlessly. "And you believed that shit? Unless you have angel or demon blood, you'll always be a pathetic scum."

"We will see demon! She only got like that after a demon scratched her. I let one scratch me, too!" Jared yells at her, lifting his shirt sleeve to reveal angry red lines where claws have split his skin, disgust clear on his face.

"The traitor is mine." My lips lift up, baring my teeth when Jared hears my words, a moment before all hell breaks loose in the forest.

Chapter Twenty-Seven

ERIC

"These can't be simple hunters." Grunting, punching the closest to me in the chest and sending him flying to a tree, I tell Raphael conversationally.

"What makes you say that?" The Archangel surprises me with his fighting skills, punching one hunter in the face before he flings him away from us.

"They've never been this strong." Ducking a swinging blade, I kick my leg out, dropping the hunter to his knees before knocking him out cold. "Or this fast."

"Huh." Demonstrating an impressive round kick, Raphael bounces on the balls of his feet while the hunter he kicked takes a few of them down with him when he drops. "I've never fought them before, so I wouldn't know."

"Ladies, if you're done chatting, we need to get the hell out of here." Maddison grabs the closest hunter's face in her hand, her red nails making it look like an alien creature is suffocating him, pushing him back so hard I'm not sure his neck didn't break.

"We need to get inside the Sanctuary." Helena is using

only her arms and legs to fight, and not the blade, to my relief. "I will not let that asshole stop me from getting Hector out." Throwing her hands outward, she sends seven hunters flying back, hitting one another. Realizing I'm watching her, she looks at me grinning. "Playtime!" Her delighted laughter makes me smile.

"Kill them!" Jared's nasally voice sounds from somewhere behind the bodies trying to overwhelm us with their numbers.

He started sounding like that after Helena punched him in the nose. Unfortunately, she didn't use her newfound strength. I'm pretty sure that was intentional, saving him for later. Maddison and I must be rubbing off on her. Even Raphael discovered his bloodlust around us, moving like a Tasmanian devil, plowing through hunters like there is no tomorrow.

"This is getting boring." Maddison does sound bored, making Helena laugh again.

A hunter uses that opportunity to blindside her, making her grunt in pain when his boot connects to her chest, and she stumbles back. Before I reach him with my claws, Helena recovers, jump kicks him in the head, and sends him flying into the group behind him. The idiots are getting themselves hurt in their desperation to get to us.

"That wasn't nice, asshole!" Chastising him, my mate punches her way through a few of them, trying to get to Jared again.

"I don't think they are trying to be nice, Helena," Raphael pipes in, taking her comment seriously, and not like the sarcasm it is.

"No, shit." Twisting away from a blade, she swings her hand in a chopping motion at the hunter's neck, incapacitating him, before kicking him on the ground. "As much fun as it is, let's deal with them later, we should really go now, I think."

I open my mouth to tell her that's what we've been trying to do when the ground beneath my feet starts shaking violently. Widening my stance for balance, I reach out to steady her, my arm freezing midair. Hunters begin shouting, some even bolting away from the woods, but I can't take my eyes away from Helena. She is still fighting, her body moving gracefully, twisting and turning like a beautiful macabre dance, dropping hunters with each movement. Her eyes are closed, a small smile playing on her lips as if she remembers fond memories. It's her power shaking the ground like Hell is trying to climb its way up. Soon, we are left alone in the woods, the quiet of the night only disturbed by stray pounding footsteps from a lost hunter on his or her way to the Sanctuary. Her eyelids flutter a heartbeat before the glowing liquid fire in her eyes zero in on my face.

"There." Dusting her hands, she beams at me. "That wasn't hard, now was it?"

"I'm not sure if I should laugh or run away screaming," Maddison mumbles under her breath, while Raphael grunts something I can't hear.

"You could've done that from the beginning, but you waited until now?" Still shaken from how powerful she is becoming by the minute, I blurt out the first thing that comes to mind.

Shrugging a shoulder, Helena looks sheepishly at me. "I didn't think of it until now."

"We better go before there is an even bigger reception party for us waiting at their doors." Shaking her head and watching Helena warily, Maddison heads towards the road.

Helena turns on her heels as well, taking the lead, striding with purpose. Raphael scurries to catch up with her, no doubt to try and tell her that her behavior is not very angelic. Snorting at my own thoughts, I grab Maddison by her arm, slowing her down. When Helena and the Archangel are ahead of us enough to not hear my words, I round on my cousin.

"And you thought it was smart to give her an unknown blade?" If I were a bull, steam would've been coming out from my nose.

"It was hers to have, Eric. Who are you to judge what she needs and doesn't need?"

My feet stop moving, uneasiness eating me inside as I watch the back of Maddison's head. She keeps walking, taking a few steps before noticing I'm not walking next to her. When she finally sees me behind her, she stops as well, turning around. We watch each other, not saying a word.

"Is this one of those things that come to you?" My fists clench in hopes she will say no. She nods once, slowly, her lips pressing into a thin, white line. "You should've told me."

"And say what exactly? I'm going to give your mate a blade before her life—" Her mouth closes with a resounding snap. Maddison closes her eyes, realizing she spoke more than she intended.

I'm in front of her before she blinks, shaking her like a rag doll in my anger. "Before her life what, Maddison?" My fingers shift into claws, piercing the skin of her arms, red blood dripping at our feet. "Speak, before I rip out your throat."

"I can't, Eric," without opening her eyes, she whispers, tears sliding down her face. "If I say a word, things will change, and I can't live knowing my big mouth caused the death of your mate. This way, she at least has a chance. I'm doing my best to stay ahead of it all, so she has a chance."

"What do you get from it?" Panting, I try to release her arms, but my hands are frozen, ready to shred skin.

"If she lives?" Finally lifting her gaze to mine, the desperation I see in her eyes sucks all the air from my lungs. "I get to live, too."

"It gets worse than what has already happened to her until now?" All I can feel is fear clawing at my insides. I'm surprised my eyes and ears are not bleeding.

"Much, much worse." At Maddison's pained whisper, I push her away from me and bolt after Helena.

Chapter Twenty-Eight

HELENA

"You don't move an inch away from her." Eric's deep voice makes me jump a foot off the ground.

Pressing a hand to my chest in a futile attempt to calm my heart, I turn to look at him. Raphael jumps back as well at the feral look on Eric's face. What could've possibly happened in the few moments after we left the woods to make him seem more demon than man? Talking to Raphael so he knows I haven't gone insane with power calmed me down, until a voice out of my nightmares messed up my fragile Zen state.

"Who poked the demon and made him feral?" Peeking around his shoulders, I search for Maddison. She must've pissed him off.

If I expected laughter, I was left disappointed.

"Did you hear what I said Archangel?" Not looking away from me, Eric resembles a gargoyle statue. The pissed off look on his face makes me want to tuck tail and run. I can only imagine how Raphael feels. Glancing at him unhinges my bottom jaw. He is scrutinizing Eric, tilting his head in a very inhuman way.

"Okay," he tells him.

"Everyone is worried about me, but I think the rest of you are going insane." Turning away from both of them, I briskly walk towards the Sanctuary. "It's like a twilight zone around all of you."

When there is no comment and a few moments have passed, I look over my shoulder. Managing to keep my face straight, I sharply turn to look in front of me. My face must be going purplish red since I'm holding my breath. It's the only thing stopping me from laughing like a crazy woman. Eric and Raphael look crazed, eyes glowing, muscles bulging from clenched fists, ready to destroy whatever enemy pissed them off. They are mumbling something, too soft for me to hear, but it can't be good because they become more animated with jerky movements with each step they take. Maddison looks like she's seen a ghost, pale with blood covering the skin on her arms. Maybe Jared's betrayal made me lose it entirely because I keep glancing behind me and find the whole thing hilarious.

The monstrosity of a building that is the Sanctuary comes into view. The old monastery, looming ahead of us like a forbidden haunted place, lures us into its gaping mouth. Forgetting all about my companions, focusing on my surroundings, I scan the area. Not a soul in sight, not even a patrol. They must be waiting to ambush us inside, and I would hate to disappoint them.

Eric and Raphael materialize on either side of me in the form of silent, glaring sentinels promising death to whoever comes near. Shaking my head at my dramatic inner voice, my fingers glide up and down the handle of the blade I tucked in the loop of my pants, a perfect holding spot for it.

The energy from the blade warms my skin so much my fingers tingle from it. I don't want to use it on the hunters, but I will if they leave me no other choice.

We stop at the open doors as one. The darkness from the inside whispers at me to turn around and leave before it's too late. Like with everything else in my life, I ignore it. Hector is somewhere inside, possibly missing a hand. The one that is acting as a decorative piece in Eric's apartment. Also, George and Cass are maybe in there too, hurt or dead. Jared looked unhinged, so I can't be sure what I'll find when I cross the threshold.

Knowing full well that I'm only stalling, I square my shoulders and, taking the few stairs two at a time, I enter the belly of the beast. Bending my knees, preparing to block a kick to the head or legs, I'm left disappointed again. No one is there, the silence of the vast place eerily making our breathing sound too loud. My eyes flick left and right, checking every shadow, all the nooks and crannies I'm familiar with that can hide a hunter.

"They couldn't have left without us seeing them." Straightening from my crouch, I turn first to Raphael, then to Eric. "They must be here." I wanted to sound sure, but the last part comes out like a question.

"They are not here, Hel." Eric keeps scanning everything around us. "I can't feel anyone here."

"I think he is right." Raphael has his hands on his hips, looking around with a frown. Maddison stays quiet.

"How's that possible, Eric?" I turn my frustration on him like it's his fault I can't find someone to hit.

"I'm not sure…" His gaze lands on mine, and the green color of his eyes bleeds through the amber glow. "But this is good." Blowing out a breath, he quickly glances at Maddison before smiling at me. "Very good!"

"Yo! Weirdo! We are here to find Hector. Remember him?" Sweeping my arm to encompass the Sanctuary acting like an abandoned tomb, I glare at him. "We can't find him if no one is here."

"We will…" Eric trails off, stiffening.

"Helena?" The voice coming from behind me stiffens my body into a rock.

I feel my blood turning cold and curdling in my veins, numbness almost dropping me on my knees. Closing my eyes, clenching my fists not to cry out in pain, I keep taking deep breaths through my nose. The organ that pumps blood into my body can't decide if it wants to beat out of my chest or shrivel and turn into a speck of dust.

"Helena?" the voice says behind me again.

Opening my eyes, the first thing I see is Eric frowning at the owner of the voice over my shoulder. Raphael's face keeps switching between wanting to look confused and incredulous. Ignoring them both, I focus on Maddison. She is not ignoring me. Her blue gaze is watching me intently, mapping out every blink of an eye, every twitch of a muscle. I feel like she reached inside my chest and ripped out my heart.

She knew!

"You can't possibly be here." Tears sliding down my face and making Maddison turn blurry, I don't turn around.

"But I'm here, Hel. Look at me."

Painfully slow, I turn around. It's like time has not passed at all. My eyes land on Amanda, my best friend, looking very much alive and well. Her hair is spiked up, as usual, blood red tips on platinum blonde hair. Her porcelain face is painted with makeup to perfection, making her brown eyes appear larger than they really are. She is as beautiful as always, dressed all in black, almost resembling a vampire with her pale skin.

"How, Amanda?" My hands tremble, and for some reason, my right hand wraps around the handle of the blade. "I saw you get killed. How are you alive?"

Her sweet, happy smile slips, and a wicked tilt of lips replaces it. Eric growls deep in his throat, his warm palm encircling half of my waist, preparing to move me out of the way if he needs to. The whooshing sound behind me to my left tells me Raphael released his wings. I'm still numb from the shock. Unmoving.

"I thought you came here for him?" Amanda clicks her fingers and Jared comes from the darkness behind her, pushing Hector in front of him.

"You are going to die for good tonight." My words hurt me more than they pain her.

Chapter Twenty-Nine

ERIC

Something is wrong with this whole picture. I still can't feel humans anywhere in the building. Quite a ridiculous thought while I'm staring at a few of them from behind Helena. Everything in me screams to push my mate behind me, protect her with my body so they must go through me if they want to hurt her. Remembering Maddison's words from earlier, I fight my instincts, staying behind Helena in hopes they'll overlook who I am.

If I'm lucky.

Raphael made all that more difficult, sprouting feathers like a peacock, but I don't let it bother me because his egotistical display hid Maddison behind him. We can use all the advantage we can get, so I'll take it. I don't even consider that he did it on purpose, not willing to give the feathered asshole too much credit. It's his kind screwing our lives up.

"Hector!" Helena tries to take a step towards her father, but I tighten my hand on her waist, halting her. "Are you okay?"

"Hel, you shouldn't be here. Run!" Hector looks horrified seeing us here, staring at Helena from his knees where Jared pushed him.

"What is the meaning of this!" Raphael packs so much power in his words I involuntarily hiss at him. Unfazed, he glares through liquid gold eyes at the hunters. "Hand over the patron this instant!"

"You lost your right to demand things from us the moment you joined them, just like you lost your path from God."

Another voice comes from the darkness behind Helena's best friend. Former best friend, I amend, because whatever this is, it's not Amanda. A man walks into view pushing the hunter, George, in front of him roughly. He looks familiar, but I can't place him until he moves his head, and the ugly scar on his face helps me remember seeing him with my mate the night Amanda was killed. Another patron. Adam, if I recall correctly. A replica of him walks out from the shadows as well, causing me to blink a few times in confusion, thinking somehow, they are messing with my head and I started seeing double. Then I notice he doesn't have a scar on his face. Twins then. I don't remember hearing his name, so I dismiss the thought.

The scarless one drags a young woman by her arm; her long, curly brown hair covering her face. Judging by everyone in attendance at this reunion, I'm guessing this is Cass, the last member from Helena's team. She whimpers when she is shoved on the ground. The floor under my feet vibrates slightly but stops so suddenly I must've imagined it. Helena says nothing, standing still, barely breathing.

"Look at us, all together again." Amanda claps her hands excitedly.

Helena tilts her head in such an animalistic way, a shiver races up and down my spine.

"I see you haven't found your sense of humor." Amanda looks disappointed.

"I lost it when my best friend died."

"I'm very much alive, thank you very much." Pursing her lips painted with black lipstick, Amanda looks petulant.

"You are something," Helena says calmly. "Alive, however, is not it. I would know."

Amanda and the creepy twins shift on their feet, coiled, ready to pounce. My hand tightens on Helena while I'm glancing at the Archangel to see if he is with the program. The shimmering gold where his eyes used to be make it difficult to judge, but I'm hoping he saw the movement. A shift of the air at my back tells me Maddison is as ready as she can be.

"Always thinking it's all about you, right Helena," Amanda snaps angrily. "The golden girl! Everything in the world revolves around her."

"You must be an idiot if that's what you think." Helena laughs, and I'm starting to wonder if maybe she is misjudging the situation. She is goading the crazy person in the room, or entryway as the case is.

"Let's see who the idiot is when I start killing them, one by one, before I end your life."

"Who are you? And why do you look like Amanda?" I want to tell Helena that no glamour can make anyone look like someone else, but I stay quiet in hopes to blend into the background.

"Ah! You still think this is a trick, huh?" Amanda curls her lips, flashing teeth. "She thinks I'm not her friend, handsome. Care to tell her how wrong she is?" Turning to glance over her shoulder, she is almost bouncing on her toes from excitement.

"Keep her talking," I whisper to my mate under my breath "She might leave your friends, and Hector, alone." Helena nods once.

"The one behind her must be rubbing off on her with his arrogance." I stiffen at the sound of his voice right before Abaddon walks up to Amanda.

"It was you that night!" Helena hisses angrily. "I thought I recognized you before I put a bullet between your eyes."

"And tonight, you'll pay for that inconvenience dearly." Abaddon grabs George by the hair, pulling him up to his feet. "First, you'll watch everyone you love die. I'll keep you for last."

"What have I ever done to you?" My mate makes me proud, staying levelheaded enough to keep them talking. Still, the moment doesn't feel right for any of us to make a move. My hand is ready to pull her back at any moment.

Until Abaddon roars a laugh and she leans back, whispering to me. "Don't pull me back, push me forward."

"No!" Hissing at her, my fingers tighten.

"It's the only way they won't expect it." Helena glances over her shoulder, not long enough to calm my anger at her demand.

"I don't need you! I just need your blood." Abaddon stops laughing long enough to share his plans. "And his too." Pointing a claw my way, all the laughter is gone from his face.

"You need my blood too now?" I chuckle, since my plan to become invisible goes down the drain. "Mighty ambitious, even for you Abaddon."

"That's because you're as ignorant as the pathetic scum

you've spent centuries protecting." Hatred burns brightly in his gaze. "With blood from both of you, I will take Lucifer's place."

"You are an idiot! No one can take his place, you moron. If he doesn't exist, his realm doesn't exist."

"Ah! But it will exist if he is still alive while I take his throne."

Helena bursts out laughing, shocking me into silence. Everyone is watching her like she is the strangest thing in this fucked up place. Slapping her hand on her thigh, bending at her waist, gasping for air, her laughter echoes around us. The waterfall of her blonde hair hides her face, and she flips it back when she straightens. A few chuckles escape her while she's trying to regain her composure. Even Abaddon watches her stupefied. Then she turns to me, there is no humor in her liquid fire gaze.

"Now, Eric."

Chapter Thirty

HELENA

My hand tightens around the hilt of the blade when Eric flings me like I weigh nothing. Sailing through the air, arching my back, I lift the dagger above my head, swinging it in an arc and embedding it right between Abaddon's eyebrows. The same spot where my bullet made a hole a few weeks ago. The sharp blade slides in like butter, and Abaddon's confused expression is the last one he makes before the symbols start glowing inside his skull. A gut-wrenching scream rips through his throat before he drops down like a tree. I ride him down to the ground like a pro surfer, pulling my blade out with a sucking sound.

Everything is frozen in place, the silence screaming at me. Looking around, I see everyone watching me in various degrees of shock. I have no idea what their problem is. I didn't do anything outwardly. I just stuck the pointy tip of a sharp object into a demon. Feeling all awkward, I wave the still glowing dagger around.

"Who's next?"

And, that's when everyone gets animated. Maybe I

should've stayed quiet, saying nothing and acting just as shocked as the rest of them. My mouth always runs amok on me. Screeching like a banshee, Amanda tackles me to the ground. I trip over Hector, hoping I didn't step on the stump where his hand used to be. Luckily, my stumble makes Jared jump away from him like a scared rabbit. Kicking her over my head, I scramble to my feet in time to see white feathers tipped in pale green wrap around Adam, effectively pushing him away from my friends. Eric plows through Solomon, claws slashing, making quick work out of him. Cass is curled up in a ball, trying to make herself as small of a target as possible, but Eric doesn't even come close to her.

Using my momentary destruction to her advantage, Amanda kicks me in the center of my chest, sending me flying back a few feet until I skid to a stop close to the still-open front doors. I can't help thinking, whatever it is that brought her back, it works well for her. Coughing out blood, lifting myself up, I grin at her. She flinches slightly, no doubt from my baring bloody teeth in her face. The doll face I've always envied on her twists into an ugly mask of rage. Hunching her shoulders and bending her head slightly down, she screams, running at me like a bull at a matador. Maddison pops out of nowhere, tripping Amanda and sending her arms cartwheeling comically before she falls down with a squeak.

"Thanks!" Grinning at her, I run to Amanda, pulling her flailing body up.

"I'm going to kill you!" Spittle flies from Amanda's lips, her body twisting this way and that as she tries to dislodge me.

"The infamous words of every dead villain, Amanda. You should know that." Dragging her by the hair, I walk closer to where Hector is still sitting on the ground and taking everything in with wide eyes.

"Hector?" Staying far enough away that Amanda can't get to him if she lessens my grip, I sweep my gaze over him. My own eyes widen when I see both his hands where they need to be. "Oh, thank God it wasn't your hand."

"What?" Eyes glazed over, he looks up at me.

"Guys! It wasn't his hand." In my excitement, I ignore Hector, yelling for the rest of them to hear my good news.

"Splendid!" Maddison is the only one as excited as me while she holds sniffling, snotty Jared by his throat pinned to the wall. I frown at Eric and Raphael.

"You can at least pretend you're happy my father didn't lose his hand, assholes." My words don't sound as badass as I was hoping because I have to struggle to keep wiggling Amanda from getting loose.

"Hel, put the blade away, would you beautiful?" Eric takes a tentative step towards me.

Frowning, I smack the hilt of the blade against Amanda's temple because my hand started getting tired from her pulling left and right constantly. She turns into a deadweight in my hand, so I drop her in a heap on the floor, still not looking away from Eric.

"I'm not the psycho here, Eric." Waving the blade in question, I point at the few remaining bad guys. "They are." I make sure I speak slowly in case his anger is messing with his head.

Maddison snickers, coughing when Eric turns his angry amber gaze her way. Raphael snorts before joining in with the coughing fit. Apparently, it's a thing now. Who knew?

"I think I'm missing something here." Lifting himself up with a groan, Hector takes a step towards me, but Eric snatches him back. What the hell is his problem?

"Hel, put the blade down. None of them are going anywhere, and your loved ones are safe." Another tentative step brings Eric closer to me.

"Monster boy, you sound like a broken record. I heard you the first time." Turning from Maddison to Raphael, I get no help in figuring out what's up his ass. "Wanna tell me what has got you all tied up in a knot?"

"You're feeling okay?" Tilting his head, he watches me intently. "I mean, like yourself."

"I'm going to have a bitch of a bruise where that thing calling herself Amanda kicked me, but apart from that, yes." Closing my eyes, I examine myself for anything unusual and come up with nothing. "Nope." Glancing back at him, I shake my head. "Same old me, the freak. I don't understand why, though."

He doesn't answer, but in the blink of an eye, he is in front of me, wrapping me in a bone-crushing hug. Chuckling, and sounding like I'm gasping for air because I am—gasping that is—I let him hold me to calm himself. Eric's body is trembling around me, and my heart melts. Whatever it is, has him really worried.

"Your eyes turn like liquid fire, especially when the blade is glowing," Maddison says from somewhere behind Eric. "It's…unsettling."

"You two sprout claws, Raphael turns into a goose, and my eyes are unsettling?" My words are muffled since my face is pressed to his chest.

Eric is chuckling, and despite myself, my lips twitch. Maddison giggles, and Raphael's deep laughter joins hers. Even Hector chuckles from somewhere, a laugh I'd recognize from miles away. This is good. It means we succeeded with one of our plans. Pulling away from Eric, I look around him. Even George and Cass look like they are smiling, although a little worse for wear.

"I'm so happy all of you are okay." Flicking my eyes to Hector's hand to reassure it's still there, my face softens at seeing him in front of me. "And with all your limbs intact, as well."

"Helena, don't move!" Maddison shout freezes me in place.

"It's good that all of you are here." Michael's voice comes from behind me, and I twist around sharply, unwilling to leave my back to the Holy asshole.

Eric hisses in pain, and I see blood welling up on his arm before sliding in rivulets down towards his fingers. I realize I nicked him with the blade when I was turning to look at Michael. Not thinking anything of it, in my haste to stop the bleeding, I cut my own finger before pressing it on his wounded skin. Fat drops of blood splatter at our feet before my skin presses to his. A wave of energy explodes from us, sending everyone flying in the air before dropping like rocks on the ground. Only me and Eric are left standing to stare at each other.

"What the hell just happened?" My words are said through a thick tongue, like I drank a bottle of vodka in one gulp. The ground under our feet feels like it's shaking, but it can also be my thundering heart trying to beat its way through my ribcage.

"I haven't the foggiest clue," Eric murmurs, looking around with a confused but wary expression on his handsome face.

Thunder booms around us, my knees buckling, but I remain standing thanks to Eric's hold on me. Lightning splits the darkness inside the sanctuary, as if we are standing in the middle of an open field while a thunderstorm is raging around us. Bright spots dance at the corners of my eyes when a familiar wave of power slams into me. I don't need to turn around to know that Michael is standing behind me in all his feathered glory.

"You two tricked me!" he roars as if we are deaf and can't hear him from a few feet away.

"No one invited you here for you to be tricked asshole," snapping angrily, I turn to look at him.

My hands might tremble from fear at seeing him almost doubled in size, lightning bolts stretching out from his wings all around us like a silver spider web. It might be fear, but I'll go with adrenaline because I need a self-esteem boost. So, I don't run away screaming. Another wave of power pulses from Michael, slamming into me, and I yelp despite my best efforts to stay quiet. Tearing of fabric mixes with the crackles of energy around us before the stinging of Michael's power is not felt on my burning skin. Wondering what caused the reprieve, I look over my shoulder before moving my whole body to fully face Eric.

Gapping like a carp out of the water, I'm unable to close my mouth. The sound of tearing fabric was his tank top turning to shreds. That's because massive black wings twice the size of the Archangels are spread out behind him, the tips of the black feathers surrounded with dancing shadows like flickering flames.

"You have wings." Playing Miss Obvious, I even point at them in case he can't feel them sticking out of his back.

"So it seems." Eric doesn't look happy about it, but I'm giddy because I want to start touching them now. "We did nothing to you, fucker." Growling over my shoulder, he addresses Michael, the pissed off Archangel I forgot all about after seeing Eric's wings. "Whatever it is you think we've done is just another reason for you to begin a fight. But this time I'll finish it."

Michael opens his mouth to say something, but we will never know what wisdom the Holy ass was going to grace us with. The ground under our feet shakes violently before splitting open. Eric throws himself back, pulling me along with him. Luckily, we land on solid ground, the hole the size of an SUV, separating us from Michael. Screams are heard from the depths, heat coming in waves and burning my skin. My body is covered in goosebumps and cold sweat drenches my body when I realize what just happened. The memory of my blood splattering on the floor before I pressed my hand on Eric's arm will haunt me forever.

In my stupidity, I opened the gate to Hell.

"I should've given you the dagger," I tell Eric through numb lips, making him grunt behind me.

"If one demon passes through that gate, I will destroy you both and the human realm." Michael's thundering voice shakes me to my core.

As if that's what they were waiting on, two wrinkly horned heads poke through the hole, glancing around. Hissing like cats, they pulled themselves out and bolted through the open doors, past the pissed off Archangel, faster than any of us can blink. Michael's roar almost makes my ears bleed.

"We need to close the damn gate, Eric." My voice is high pitched, but I don't care.

"We can only close it from the other side." Eric's words sound hollow and numb.

Lightning bolts start crashing around us as Michael tries his best to skewer us where we are still sitting on the floor. Somewhere behind us, I can hear the others coming around after being unconscious from the hit they took. I can't even spare them a glance. Michael, knowing that Eric is blocking his power, gets more pissed off by the second.

Maddison crawls over to us, still looking like she just walked out of a photo shoot. Her face is grim, and a look passes between her and Eric that makes me want to puke. Did they know something like this could happen? Why didn't anyone tell me? Maybe then, I wouldn't have touched the damn blade to begin with. Hector comes near us as well, a lump forming in my throat at how frail and beaten he is. Michael's words echo in my head. 'I'll destroy you and this entire realm.'

"Let's do it, Eric." I want to run and hide, everything in me rebelling against stepping one foot in Hell, but innocent humans will die if I don't. My eyes focus pleadingly on Maddison.

"I'll look after all of them until you two come back." Turning her gaze to Eric, she sets her mouth in a firm line. "And you better come back. Fast!"

"Amanda…" my words trail off.

"I'll keep her away from everyone until you get back." She promises. "You two worry about coming back, leave the rest to me."

After a moment, Eric nods once, standing up and pulling my numb body with him. We step closer to the hole, radiating heat in unbearable levels. My heart shrinks, trying to hide. I want to hide too, but instead I step next to Eric bravely, even while I'm screaming inside.

"We will be fine." Saying it out loud makes me almost believe it. "Get in, get out, go home." I see Eric reluctantly open his mouth, and I panic. "Now is not the time to develop angelic traits, asshole. You better lie to me and be damn good about it!"

"We will be fine." Dutifully, like any man should be

when his woman is on the verge of a nervous breakdown, Eric reassures me.

"Thanks!" Smiling at him, I take his hand. He nods once jerkily, but I ignore that. It can't be that bad, right?

Right?

Closing my eyes, I take the step off the ledge. My body feels weightless for a second, clutching Eric with one hand and the damn dagger in the other. The menacing chuckle that freezes the blood in my veins must've been my imagination before we plunge into the depths of Hell.

vinci-books.com/encounterdevil

Cheating the Devil? Fun. Getting caught? Not so much.

I escaped death, but now I'm the grand prize in a supernatural free-for-all. Angels lie, demons manipulate, and my only way out is through Hell—literally. Lucky me, I've got Eric, Prince of Hell, at my side. Unlucky for everyone else, I don't play fair.

Turn the page for a free preview…

Encounter with the Devil: Chapter One

HELENA

The slight breeze, a faint scent of caramel making my mouth water, and the silvery moonlight were not the things I expected to see when dropping down to Hell, unannounced. After falling through an endless abyss for what felt like hours, my body passed through an invisible barrier before my tailbone took the brunt of the impact when I hit the packed-dirt ground. For whatever reason, I expected to jump in the gaping hole in the middle of Sanctuary and fall to the center of the Earth with lava licking at my heels.

As you might suspect by now, that is not the case.

Glancing at Eric from the corner of my eye tells me I'm still missing something. The unease is made stronger by the gnawing feeling in my gut and the involuntary tremble in my hands.

Holy shit, I'm in Hell!

My mind screams like that annoying girl in a horror movie, the one we all want to tell to shut up, while my body is standing as still as a statue expecting an attack at any moment. You can't just decide to drop in here and no one to notice, right?

"You okay?" Reaching for me, Eric tucks me under his shoulder. "You seem shocked."

"Ummm…kinda." With great effort, I pull my gaze away from my surroundings to look at him. "I'm not sure what I was expecting, but this"—Waving a hand to encompass everything, I let it drop to my side limply—"was not it."

"No, pitchforks?" Chuckling, his green eyes dance with amusement.

"No, no pitchforks." My snickering sounds strained. "Now what?"

He does a visual inspection while lines form in neat rows on his forehead. "We ended up further from the portal that we passed through than I expected." Rubbing the back of his neck, his frown deepens." I was too worried about you to pay closer attention. It must've picked up on my bloodline and spit us out here."

"That's a good thing or a bad thing?" Gut tightening, my head swivels left and right, expecting a horde of demons to descend on us at any moment. "Your face is not giving me the warm fuzzies right now."

Lips quirking on one side, Eric looks down at me. "I thought you liked my face."

"Just 'cause you are pretty doesn't mean I'm all happy to get my butt handed to me here." His grin grows, and my hand itches to smack it off him. "Plus, you are stalling. Where are we, and how do we get out of here?"

"You picked up on that, huh." With a sigh, he turns in half a circle. "We need to head north. At the moment, we are too close to Lucifer's quarters. I would rather be away from here before he senses my presence."

"Why are we standing here, chatting? Let's go." Pulling away from him, picking a direction, my feet move fast.

"Aren't you forgetting something?"

Turning around, I keep walking backward with an eyebrow raised in question. Eric points to his right, and I follow the direction of his finger. My ability to see in the dark is not as good as his, but there is no mistaking the glint of the blade reflecting the glow of the moon. My feet stop like they've been nailed on the packed dirt, the bottom of my stomach dropping. A quick glance tells me Eric is forcing himself to stay rooted to the spot, his outstretched arm slightly twitching from the effort. Unwilling to test theories or ask questions when all I want to do is get out of here, my body moves so fast I'm almost sprinting. Snatching the dagger, tucking it at the small of my back, I turn to him.

"Got it, let's go."

His mouth opens, whatever he was about to say lost in the sharp intake of breath, and his head snaps to his left, I'm surprised I didn't hear his neck breaking. Amber overtakes the green color of his eyes, and the unnatural stiffening of his body causes alarms to blare in my head. My own questions get strangled, forming a lump in my throat when a whooshing sound like helicopter blades reaches my ears.

They have helicopters in Hell? my mind supplies right before I'm tackled to the ground.

With a loud oomph, all the oxygen exits my lungs, my head spinning when Eric rolls us to the nearest tree. The blade digs into the skin of my back, luckily not severing my spine. Ending up on top of Eric at the gnarled roots of an ancient tree, I lift my head, pushing the hair out of my face. The area where we were standing looks like a circle clearing, surrounded by thorned bushes and rock formations I didn't pay close attention to until now. From the place where I'm sprawled on top of a firm, warm body, I can tell it was made on purpose, not a natural formation as I previously assumed. Gray swirls resembling some of the markings on my blade are etched into the rocks, forming a tribal-looking art around the empty space in the middle. Ancient trees surround it on three sides, leaving the front open to a vast horizon reminding me of old Earth. A time when technology and people haven't destroyed the beauty of nature around us. Dirt paths spread through tall trees, splitting in different directions, like veins forking under pale skin. The bright silver glow makes everything look enchanted, sparkling like jewels under the giant full orb in the sky. A starless sky, now that I'm focused on it.

Eric pulls me closer, wrapping his large hand at the back of my head, pressing my face in the crook of his neck. His arms are like steel bands around me, the stiffness more noticeable now that I'm touching him. My stupid body doesn't understand the panic that is filling my every pore. Eric is still shirtless from his wings bursting out of his back before we ended up in this mess. I become acutely aware of hard planes and muscles pressed to me from shoulder to groin, his hips wedged between my spread thighs. Warmth pools in my lower belly, and the scent of his skin where my nose is pressed to his neck hitches my breath.

I'm acutely aware of the moment his breath stops, his attention turning from whatever made him put us in this position to me. A deep rumble vibrates from his chest to mine, and I can hear him sniffing me. "Bad timing, Hel. Tone it down, or we might get caught with me buried inside you."

That's one way to throw a bucket of ice-cold water on a girl's libido. Muscles clenching in anticipation of whatever he sensed coming for us, I jerk my head up, but he holds me firmly where I am.

"No one wants to get caught with their pants around their ankles." My words are muffled, the chuckle falling flat. "You need to find a shirt to put on."

"Right after I get us out of here." His whispered promise is met with a louder whooshing sound.

The temperature around us goes up by a few degrees. Sweat starts trickling between my shoulder blades, my hair plastering on my skin and Eric's shoulders. Blasts of hot air keep hitting my back in waves and the strangest thought barrels through my head. *Why am I on top of Eric? He always shields me using his own body. Now it seems like he is using me for a living shield.* Pushing the stupid idea to the back of my mind, I strain my ears to decipher what's making the sound.

Whoosh, whoosh, whoosh.

There is a pause between the sound and the blast of scorching heath burning every inch of exposed skin. If it keeps going, I have no doubt I'm going to blister from head to toe. Heart jackhammering in sync with the men underneath me, I grind my teeth so I don't utter a sound. It's not every day I see Eric hiding instead of bulldozing his way through whatever stands in his way. That's enough to hold me frozen, even if it means I'll burn to a crisp under the barrage of what feels like an open furnace at my back.

After a long time, when I'm sure I'll be spending days laying on my stomach to protect my burned back, the heat starts dissipating along with the whooshing sound that is getting further away from us. Eric loosens his hold on me but doesn't push me off him. Curiosity is stronger than the agonizing pain in my back, and with great effort, I lift my head, looking up where I can see the starless sky. A shadow large enough to almost cover the entire span of the pregnant silver moon makes me suck in a sharp breath. I regret it the same second when an excruciating stinging pain stabs my back. Regardless of it all, my eyes must be as round and as big as the moon above me. After the shadow banks left and disappears in the distance, my stunned gaze drops down to Eric. He is watching me like he expects me to pull my blade and cut his throat. Swallowing the bile that's trying to push its way through my esophagus, my eyes lift up to where I saw the shadow last.

Hell has motherfucking dragons. More extensive than a helicopter, with a fire burning along their spine and wings type of dragons.

And no one thought this little information to be significant enough to be the first thing they mentioned.

Grab your copy...
vinci-books.com/encounterdevil

About the Author

Maya Daniels, USA Today Bestselling and multi-award-winning supernatural suspense author, is a fun-loving woman with many talents.

She traveled the world, gaining life experiences that helped her career as an investigative journalist, as well as her storytelling. Maya writes compelling tales of magic, mythical creatures, loyalty, and life-changing friendships with snarky female characters—much like herself.

Her travels have taken her to Europe, Africa, Asia, Australia, and America. Born with her feet in motion, she currently resides in Ohio, spinning her next epic story that you will not want to put down.

Her biggest 'sins' are her love of chocolate and coffee—through an IV drip! One to never sit still, Maya practices Reiki healing, different types of martial arts, reads about the arcane, talks to furry creatures more than humans, picks up a sledgehammer for home improvement, and travels with her fated mate, seeking her own adventures.